BASSETS AND BLACKMAIL

BASSETS AND BLACKMAIL

A DOG DETECTIVE SERIES

SANDRA BAUBLITZ

This is a work of fiction. Names, places, businesses, and people are the imagination of the author and fictitious. Any resemblance to actual people (living or dead), places, or names/businesses is purely coincidental.

BASSETS AND BLACKMAIL

ISBN: **978-1720505228**

Author website: www.sandrabaublitz.com

Cover art by SwoonWorthy Book Covers

www.bookcover-designs.blogspot.com

V1

❀ Created with Vellum

ACKNOWLEDGMENTS

The author wishes to thank her wonderful cover designer Sherry Soule of Swoonworthy Book Covers and her fantastic beta readers: Anne, Babs, Dena, Jane, Jeannie, Kristin, Mary, and Sandy.

And a special thank you to Nancy Bober, audiobook narrator extraordinaire.

For Paw's fans.

"Dog Detective Rule #2: Don't be too proud to accept assistance from your friends – even if they are a cat."

- The Dog Detective

CAST OF CHARACTERS

Clarissa Hayes – Freelance writer and amateur sleuth. Owner of Paw. Bruce's girlfriend. She's acting in the mystery game. Will she stumble onto another murder investigation?

Paudius Pernivious (aka Paw) – Clarissa's Saint Bernard. Mischievous, loyal, and lovable. Will he sniff out the clues to a crime?

Bruce Sever — Clarissa's private detective boyfriend. He's once again drawn into a mystery.

Shelbee Van Vight – One of Clarissa's best friends. Animal-lover and respected pet-sitter. Owner of Samuel and Bitsy. She's assisting Robert and Jac in preparing the mystery game. Helps Clarissa in her sleuthing.

Samuel – Shelbee's mastiff. He's best friends with Paw. He's helped Paw solve a previous mystery.

Bitsy – Shelbee's Pomeranian. Rescued in one of Clarissa's previous murder investigations. Paw doesn't trust Pomeranians, so they have a strained relationship.

Jacqueline (Jac) Weldon – One of Clarissa's best friends. She's playing in the murder mystery game and has assisted Clarissa in her prior mysteries. She's close friends with the Innsmans.

Robert Roberts – Local actor and friends with Clarissa, Shelbee, and Jac. He's playing the main role in the mystery game. Owner of Kathleen and Pedro.

Kathleen – Robert's gray-and-black-striped cat. Friends with Paw.

Pedro – Robert's parrot. He loves to talk.

William Innsman – Husband of Patricia Innsman. Co-owner and innkeeper of Peaceful Dreams Bed and Breakfast. Owner of Henry. What dark secrets are in his past?

Patricia Innsman – Wife of William Innsman. Co-owner and innkeeper of Peaceful Dreams. Owner of Henry. What will she do to protect her husband?

Henry – Basset hound puppy who has diabetes. Owned by William and Patricia Innsman. Friends with Paw and the other animals. What will his excellent nose sniff out?

Rascal – Cat. Henry's best friend. Owned by William and Patricia. Gets along with other animals.

Harry – Chief of police of Tranquil Valley. Uncle to Clarissa. Tough and often grumpy but has a heart of gold. Wants Clarissa to avoid crime but respects her insights.

Alma – Harry's wife and former secretary.

Hal McFarlane – Coroner/medical examiner. Good friends with Harry.

Lillian Hardcastle – Elderly neighbor and friend of Clarissa's. Speaks her mind. Owner of Saber. She has a mystery to solve with Clarissa's help.

Saber – Lillian's black cat. He is as stubborn and grumpy as his owner and finds his own mystery.

Donna Dayton – Wife of James Dayton. Guest at Peaceful Dreams. She came for a mystery game, but will she find a murder instead? And did she have a past with the dead man?

James Dayton – Husband of Donna Dayton. Guest at Peaceful Dreams. Drinks too much. He has a confrontation with the man who dies. Did he murder him?

Madeline Wells – Guest at Peaceful Dreams. Friends with Karen Taylor. She loves to play murder mystery games, but did she murder the dead man?

Karen Taylor – Guest at Peaceful Dreams. Friends with Madeline Wells. She humors Madeline by playing murder mystery games, but is there another reason she agreed to come to the bed and breakfast?

Jessica St. Clair – Guest at Peaceful Dreams. Girlfriend to Thomas Cafferty. She claims Thomas was murdered. Was he? And was she responsible?

Thomas Cafferty – Guest at Peaceful Dreams. Jessica St. Clair is his companion. Irascible and argumentative. Why did he come for a murder mystery game? And who killed him?

Kara – Young girl who lives in Tranquil Valley. She features in Saber's mystery.

Kara's mom – She features in Saber's mystery.

Dana Harford – What does she know about Saber's collar?

Mark Carter – Local newspaper reporter. He asks some pointed questions. Determined to find out information for his news story.

Officer Steven Heldman – One of Harry's police officers.

Officer Banks – Another of Harry's police officers.

Officer Rob Barnes – Another of Harry's police officers.

CHAPTER 1

Clink! Clink!

William Innsman tapped his spoon against his wine glass and raised it for a toast. "To the very first Peaceful Dreams Murder Mystery Game. May you all find the clues before the murderer finds you."

Muted chuckles and murmurs of "Hear! Hear!" issued from the guests seated around the dining table in the Peaceful Dreams Bed and Breakfast.

Thomas Cafferty scowled at his wine.

James Dayton took a deep drink and raised his glass in the air, saying, "And to our lovely innkeepers, Patricia and William."

Everyone raised their glasses and smiled, except for Cafferty.

"Thank you. As you no doubt know, I always say that

with a name like Innsman, I had to become an innkeeper."

Many of the guests laughed, while some rolled their eyes.

Patricia groaned, shaking her head.

Donna Dayton leaned forward. "William, won't you tell us how you came to find such a lovely old building to refurbish into Peaceful Dreams?"

William grinned. "I would be delighted. Patricia and I love to hunt for old things to repurpose. We were on our way to a flea market when a truck dumped a load of logs across the road. The police directed us to an alternate route that took us through Tranquil Valley. As we crested the hill outside, I spied this old house. Patricia gasped and ordered me to the side of the road."

Patricia huffed, wearing a grin. "I did not. You were pulling over before I opened my mouth."

He winked at her. "Yes, dear." William teased back. "But I can read your mind."

Patricia shook her head in good-natured exasperation at her husband of ten years. They were a charming couple in their mid-fifties, having found each other later in life. Love shone through their eyes whenever they looked at each other. William was a tall man, standing over six feet tall, with salt-and-pepper hair and kind gray eyes. Patricia was tall for a woman, with chestnut hair and warm brown eyes. The couple exuded kindness and good humor.

William explained to Donna, "We took one look at the

house and contacted the real estate agent. It was easy to purchase, having sat vacant for several years. Then the refurb work began."

He continued to explain, but I tuned out as I had heard the story many times and had even helped with the work on a small scale.

Instead, I turned to Patricia sitting on my right and asked, "How is Henry?"

Henry was the Innsman's basset hound. He had the big, sad eyes of the breed and loved attention. Normally he followed either Patricia or William everywhere, but for the dinner party, Patricia sequestered him in the kitchen with the rest of the pets. They included my Saint Bernard, Paw, and my best friend Shelbee's dogs, Samuel, a mastiff, and Bitsy, a Pomeranian. Patricia's cat, Rascal, and Robert's cat, Kathleen, were there too. Robert Roberts, whose name always elicited a laugh, was seated across from me at the dinner table and would be a prominent player in the murder mystery game.

Patricia smiled. "Henry is doing much better. The vet says his diabetes is under control. She complimented me on how well he's doing." Her smile faded. "I still can't believe that someone would abandon him because of his health problem. He's only a puppy."

Patricia and William had found Henry, three months old at the time, in a shelter and rescued him days from being put down. Now, six months later and with wonderful care lavished on him by his new family, Henry was a happy puppy. He had been born with diabetes, and his previous owner didn't want the bother of his care. Patricia, however, prepared special meals for him and diligently gave him his prescribed medicines.

"How are Rascal and Henry getting along?"

Patricia laughed. "They're best friends now. You'd never have guessed it at first. Rascal hissed and spat when Henry first came here, but now he loves to cuddle with him. Yesterday he groomed Henry."

I smiled. "That's wonderful. They're such lovable guys."

"So is Paw, Clarissa."

"When he's not getting into trouble."

Paw is my Saint Bernard, Paudius Pernivious, who loved to dig, hence his nickname, Paw. I loved him dearly. One thing he loved more than digging was investigating mysteries. As did I. We'd both fell into solving crimes through a series of mysteries involving our friends and family.

Shelbee spoke from across the table. "Clarissa Hayes."

I turned, curious why she was using my full name.

Shelbee was gesturing to me but speaking to the woman on her right.

I nodded to the woman who was dressed in a light blue pantsuit with a flower in her light brown hair. The woman waved to me.

Shelbee completed the introduction. "Clarissa, this is Madeline Wells. She and her friend, Karen Taylor, are eager for the mystery to begin."

Karen Taylor wore a stylish gray wool suit; her chestnut-streaked hair pulled back low on her neck in a chignon. She nodded to me. “Nice to meet you.”

“And you both as well. Have either of you participated in a mystery game before?”

Madeline's smile widened. “Lots of them. We love murder mysteries. Shelbee tells us that you have solved real crimes.”

I shifted in my seat, self-conscious at the attention. “A few.”

Shelbee grinned and winked at me. “Clarissa's boyfriend is a detective.”

Karen and Madeline goggled at me.

I scowled at Shelbee who continued to grin. “Yes. He is.”

“She's worked with him on cases,” Shelbee added.

Both women leaned forward as Madeline said, “That must be exciting.”

“At times,” I said, not wanting to encourage them.

Bruce Sever, my detective boyfriend, didn't like to talk about his work since he took client confidentiality seriously. I wished he were here now to deflect the women's interest, but he was out of town visiting friends. Bruce and I had met when I found a dead body in my neighbor's shed.

Madeline Wells leaned so far forward, she grazed her plate with her chest. “Do you go on stake-outs?”

Shelbee took pity on me. “She has a time or two, but they're really boring.”

Thomas Cafferty spoke loudly, cutting through the conversations around the table. “This wine is garbage.”

His female companion, Jessica, whose last name I hadn’t heard, rolled her eyes at his rude pronouncement. I didn’t know if she was his wife or girlfriend since Cafferty just referred to her as Jessica or honey.

Various guests gasped or glared at Cafferty. Patricia drew in her breath beside me.

Not being a wine fan, I had opted for water at dinner, but in my opinion, it was rude to insult your host's selections at a meal.

We all turned to observe William's reaction. To my surprise, he smiled and dipped his head. “Well...I wouldn't call it garbage, but I admit it isn't the finest wine available since we’re on a budget being a new inn.” He shrugged. “We usually only serve breakfast. To celebrate our first murder mystery, we decided to offer dinner. Wine seemed appropriate under the circumstances. You see when we refurbished this house, we discovered several bottles of wine in the basement.”

By now, everyone but Cafferty was hanging on William's every word. “Cheap dreck, no doubt.”

I heard a squeak and turned to see Donna Dayton, who sat on my left, shift in her chair. Jessica, sitting on Cafferty’s right, fiddled with her spoon.

William shrugged. “Most were, except for one special bottle.” William paused to build suspense.

On his right, Robert Roberts was poised on the edge

of his seat. No doubt he would be urging William to join the theater.

Jac, beside Robert, leaned forward.

William bent down next to his chair. I had seen him place a canvas bag next to it when we sat down for the meal. He sat up, lifting a wine bottle onto the table.

Cafferty sat up, exclaiming, "Impossible!"

Donna Dayton half stood, saying, "Oh my gosh!"

I was confused. I turned to Patricia who sat back and gave me a small smile. I knew nothing about wine. I didn't tolerate alcohol well, so I seldom drank it.

Cafferty huffed. "That can't be real!"

William smirked. "I assure you this wine is the real thing."

Donna's voice squeaked. "That's a Chateau Haut-Brion."

"Yes." William nodded. "An excellent vintage too."

Donna dropped back into her seat, shaking her head.

Cafferty snorted. "Impossible. That wine has to be vinegar by now after being stored in the basement."

William smirked. "Maybe it is. Maybe it isn't. Our local wine expert believes it has value so next month I'm donating it to be auctioned off for the fundraiser for our local park. The proceeds will go to rebuilding the park's gazebo."

Cafferty shook his head, disgust on his face. "You're an idiot!"

William stiffened. "There's nothing idiotic about charity."

"There is if you're giving away something valuable."

Both men glared at each other.

Robert cleared his throat, raising his glass, and stood. "A toast to fine wines and good taste."

Everyone but William and Cafferty raised their glasses. Patricia reached across the table and laid her hand on William's arm. He shook himself then picked up the bottle of wine and stood. "If you'll excuse me, I'll return this to the wine cellar."

As William stood up, Cafferty shoved back his chair, saying, "Fine wine? This stuff isn't fine. It's dreck." He threw down his napkin, jerked his head at Jessica, and stalked out of the room.

Jessica plopped down her glass and hurried after him.

William strode after them turning left at the door.

No one said anything for a minute then James turned to Patricia. "You have a wine cellar?"

Patricia grimaced. "We have racks in the basement to hold our small wine selection. William calls it his wine cellar."

"I'd love to see it."

"Ask William tomorrow. I'm sure he'll show it to you."

Jac, one of my best friends, sat next to Robert. "If William wants to build a real wine cellar, just call Dad. He'll help." Her dad was a self-taught handyman who had been fixing up their house. He had helped William on several projects around the bed and breakfast.

Patricia smiled. "Thank you, Jac. William and I appreciate all you and your dad have done to help out."

Jac nodded.

Madeline Wells spoke to Patricia. "When will we start the mystery game?"

Her friend nudged her. "Not now, Madeline."

Patricia waved Karen's admonishment aside. "It's all right. The game begins first thing tomorrow morning. While we've been eating, an envelope with your identities, a clue, and the game rules have been slipped under the doors to each of your rooms. We've hidden clues around the bed and breakfast for you to find. We'll assemble here over breakfast to clarify any questions you have then the game will begin."

Madeline smiled, nudging Karen, and stood up. "We'll retire now and wish you a good night."

Karen shook her head, wearing a bemused smile. "Thank you for a lovely meal, Mrs. Innsman. We look forward to tomorrow."

Madeline urged her friend to hurry from the room.

Donna Dayton stared after the retreating women. Clearing her throat, she said, "We should go up to bed too. Thank you for a delicious meal." She stood up, staring down at her husband.

James gulped the last of his wine and rose slowly. He stared at the bottle sitting on the table in front of him.

Patricia gestured to the bottle. "You're welcome to take the bottle up to your room, Mr. Dayton."

Donna frowned, but James grabbed the bottle with a "Thank you."

Together the couple walked out of the room and climbed the stairs.

Jac stood and stretched. “I'll clear the dishes.”

Shelbee stacked Robert's plate on top of hers. “I'll help. I want to check on the animals in the private kitchen too.”

Patricia demurred. “You ladies don't have to help. You've already done so much.”

“No problem,” Jac assured her.

I patted Patricia's hand. “We love to help.” To Shelbee and Jac, I said, “I'll help clear then walk the dogs before I head home with Paw.”

Robert stood, rounded the table, and pulled out Patricia's chair. “You, lovely lady, must rest. You've had a busy day.”

“Robert,” Patricia said, “you are a true gentleman, but I still have lots to do for tomorrow's game.”

“Not to worry, Patricia, we have it covered. The game plans are set, and the girls and I will take care of last minute details.”

Shelbee, Jac, and I nodded. “We have it under control,” Jac spoke for all three of us.

Patricia smiled. “Thank you, dears. I'll leave it in your capable hands and go find William.”

She walked from the room and turned toward the basement where William was returning his bottle of wine.

Robert glanced at me. “I'll help you walk the dogs.”

I nodded, glad for the help.

The four of us cleared the table, carrying dishes through the connecting door between the dining room and the B and B's commercial kitchen. Once the table was cleared, we crossed the hall to the Innsman's private kitchen where we were met by the animal brigade. Due to health department regulations, the B and B required separate kitchens to serve food.

Paw, Samuel, and Bitsy greeted us in a chorus of barks and yips with wagging tails. Henry bayed, delighted to see us. Shelbee gently shushed them, concerned that they would disturb the guests. Kathleen, a long-haired, gray and black-striped tabby, wound around Robert's legs as Rascal sat tall and proud on the kitchen counter.

As I bent to kiss Paw on his head and scruff his neck, he looked up and slurped my face.

Jac and Shelbee laughed at me.

Robert picked up Kathleen and cuddled her. "How is my little kotyonok?" Robert had Russian heritage and kotyonok, which meant kitten, was his term of endearment for Kathleen. "Have you had fun visiting your friends?"

Mrrr.

She nuzzled his chin.

"I bet you miss your friend, Pedro."

Purr. Purr.

Robert smiled as he caressed her fur. Pedro was Robert's talking parrot. Surprisingly, he and Kathleen were great companions.

Shelbee picked up Bitsy. "Hey, Sweetkins. Did you and

Samuel have a good visit with Paw, Henry, and the kitties?"

Paw whined. Shelbee was working with him to get him to accept Bitsy since he hated Pomeranians. My big, tough Saint Bernard once had a neighboring Pomeranian who had terrorized him. Ever since Paw hated Poms. Now that Shelbee sheltered Bitsy, she and I were working to train the dogs to accept each other. The fact that they stayed in the kitchen without incident was a good sign.

Bitsy came to live with Shelbee after events during our last investigation at a local dog show. Samuel, a mastiff, had been part of the dog show and was adopted by Shelbee. He leaned against her side, tongue lolling out in bliss.

Rascal, his cream-colored fur and brown ears and tail gleaming under the kitchen lights, observed from a safe distance. Henry walked over and sat on my foot. He and Paw adored each other.

Jac picked up Rascal and cuddled him. Rascal liked us but adored Jac. She scratched his chin.

"Purr. Purr."

Shelbee placed Bitsy on the floor. "Well, guys, those dishes won't wash themselves."

I snapped on Paw's leash. "Robert and I will take the dogs for a walk while you start on the dishes."

Robert snapped leashes on Samuel and Bitsy. Both dogs wiggled, eager to take a walk. I snapped the final leash on Henry. He stood, tail wagging. Paw led the way, pulling me to the kitchen door. Once outside the dogs pulled on their leashes, headed for the garden out back.

The Peaceful Dreams Bed and Breakfast sat on a hill on the south side of our town, Tranquil Valley. The house rose three stories into the early autumn sky. Darkness was descending, cloaking the house in shadows. Dormer windows jutted from the third-floor roofline where the Innsmans resided in their private apartment. A small bedroom for private guests and a storage room completed the floor plan.

The kitchens, dining room, and living room took up the first floor. A beautiful, newly refurbished staircase ascended from the foyer up through the second and to the third floors.

The second floor was designated for paying guests. The former master suite which was to the right of the second-floor landing contained a large bed plus an additional attached bath and sitting area. Thomas Cafferty and Jessica resided in this room.

The Daytons were staying in the first room to the left of the landing across the hall from the room Karen Taylor and Madeline shared. These rooms shared connecting baths to their neighbor.

The Daytons' room connected to Robert's. He was staying at the inn since there was room from a last-minute cancellation. The fifth room was unoccupied, due to unexpected minor repairs. Karen and Madeline were fortunate as it allowed them to have the connecting bathroom to themselves.

Robert took a deep breath. "Ah. I do love the smell of autumn."

Samuel raised his nose, sniffing the air. A chittering sound came from a nearby maple tree. Samuel lunged toward the tree, Robert holding tight to the leash while Bitsy yipped and danced. A squirrel poked its head above the foliage, tempting Samuel to chase him.

Fortunately for me, Paw regarded the squirrel with dispassion. Instead, he trailed a scent in the opposite direction of the tree.

"Woo. Woo." Henry bayed at the squirrel then swung his head to watch Paw. He turned back to the squirrel then put his nose to the ground and followed the same scent Paw was tracking.

Samuel whined.

Robert patted his back. "Sorry, Sammy, but that squirrel is out of reach. Best to ignore him."

Samuel growled at the squirrel then allowed Robert to tug him after Paw.

"Yip. Yip." Bitsy turned and followed Samuel.

I trotted to keep up with Paw and Henry who were racing to find the source of the scent. Both dogs pulled me through the garden. "Easy, guys."

They halted at the base of a rhododendron. I heard rustling then a brown blur with a white cotton ball tail shot from under the bush.

Both dogs lunged, knocking me to my knees.

Robert grabbed the leashes before I lost my grip. He struggled to maintain a hold on all four dogs.

A voice called, "I got it!" Donna Dayton ran to Robert's side and grabbed the leashes for Paw and Henry. Together they controlled the dogs.

I stood and grasped Paw's collar. "Easy, big guy. That rabbit is long gone."

Paw gave a soft "woof" and stared pointedly at me. "Yes. It probably is my fault you didn't catch him, but you've had a good dinner. Far better than a rabbit."

He regarded me with skepticism clearly doubting my assertion. I gave him a big hug and he sat at my feet, wagging his tail.

Henry continued to sniff the ground, letting out a soft "woo-woo."

I smiled at Donna. "Thank you so much. I'd hate to think how long we would have chased the dogs if they had trailed that rabbit."

Donna waved her hand in the air. "No problem. I used to have a bloodhound, so I know what you mean."

Samuel sniffed the ground around Robert's feet, but Bitsy stood up against Donna's leg.

"Hi, there sweetie. Aren't you just adorable?"

Bitsy yipped and wiggled at the compliment.

Robert laughed. "Looks like you made a friend."

Donna smiled down at Bitsy. "I'm honored." She glanced up at Robert. "You are part of the murder mystery, aren't you?"

Robert nodded. "Yes." Tipping his head to me, he said, "We both are."

I demurred. "Robert is too kind. He has a major part

to play. I have one line which suits me fine. Robert is the star of our local theater."

Donna bent to pet Bitsy. "Are you a professional actor?"

"I used to be." Robert shrugged. "Now I am content to teach acting and produce when I can. The local theater is a pleasure to act in as is this murder mystery."

Donna stood up. "I don't suppose you would divulge any clues in the game."

"No way." Robert winked. "That would spoil the fun."

A voice by the house yelled, "You are despicable. How dare you accuse me of that?"

A second voice sneered. "I accuse you because it's true. You are too drunk to realize it."

CHAPTER 2

Startled, the dogs lifted their heads, perked their ears, and stared through the growing darkness toward the house. Stars had begun to appear in the night sky.

The male voices were familiar. One belonged to James Dayton. The other was Thomas Cafferty.

Donna gasped. "Excuse me." She hurried toward the men.

"James," she called, "what's wrong?"

Paw stood, growled low, and pulled on his leash to follow Donna, as did Samuel.

Robert tipped his head to indicate we should follow. I agreed and the six of us walked toward the voices.

With slurred speech, James said, "Stay out of this, Donna. Cafferty, you're a piece of garbage. No one is going to believe what you say."

Cafferty ignored him and focused on Donna. "Ah, your lovely wife. Perhaps we should discuss her criminal failings instead."

James swung at Cafferty, punching him in the jaw and sending him staggering back. James staggered too from the force of his swing. A strong scent of alcohol wafted our way.

Donna clung to him as she attempted to control him.

Cafferty regained his balance and smirked. "You've just proven my point."

Paw pushed between the men with Samuel by his side. A low growl came from both dogs.

Cafferty looked down and raised his hand as though preparing to strike the dogs.

"Don't you dare!"

He glared at my command but lowered his arm.

Henry and Bitsy woofed and yipped but stood by my feet.

Robert shifted to stand in front of me while facing both men, holding tight to the dogs' leashes. "I suggest you return to your rooms and calm down."

Donna grasped her husband's arm. "We'll do that." She nudged James back toward the French doors opening onto the garden.

James protested. "I have more to say."

Robert swung his head toward James. "Not tonight." Samuel and Paw remained focused on Cafferty.

"Come on, James," Donna urged.

I whispered to her, "Will you be all right?"

She nodded with a grimace.

James sneered at Cafferty. "This isn't over." Then wobbled alongside his wife as she led him into the house.

Cafferty smirked. "Some guests are rude, wouldn't you say?"

Robert looked him up and down. "Yes. I would."

Cafferty scowled. "I'd watch what I said theater man. We all have sins to be unveiled." He addressed me. "Call off your dog before I report him to animal control for threatening me."

"Threatening you? Ha. You, sir, have not been threatened."

Paw growled and stepped forward a pace.

Robert touched my arm. "Call Paw back, Clarissa."

"Paw, Samuel, come here guys."

Both dogs swung their heads toward me, then gave one final long stare at Cafferty before trotting over to me.

Cafferty smirked, turned, and sauntered back into the house through the French doors.

I made a mental note to be sure to close and lock the doors before I left for the night.

"Are you all right?" Robert asked me.

"Yes, but I wonder what that was all about."

He shrugged. "Who knows? I don't like either man to be honest. Remind me to suggest Shelbee and Jac lock their door tonight."

"Good idea. We'd best get back and see if we can help in the kitchen."

Robert nodded and urged the dogs back to the private kitchen.

Robert ushered me through the door as the dogs pushed ahead.

Samuel rushed to Shelbee's side where she stood at the counter, pulling down a tin of cocoa.

"Hey, sweetie, how are you? Did you have a good walk?"

Bitsy ran to her and stood up on her leg, yipping excitedly.

"Hi, sweetheart." She blew kisses to the little dog as she measured cocoa into a cup. Holding up the tin, she asked, "Want some?

"No. Thank you," I said and glanced over my shoulder to see Robert shake his head in the negative.

Kathleen and Rascal sat together on the kitchen island, observing Shelbee. Robert joined them and stroked Kathleen's fur. Rascal head-butted Robert for attention and Robert obliged.

Henry waddled over to his water bowl and took a long drink while Paw leaned against my side.

I scratched his head. "We had some excitement outside."

Jac entered the kitchen with a bowl of leftovers in time to hear me. She opened the fridge door, asking, "What excitement? Did the dogs see Clarence?"

"Who's Clarence?" Both Robert and I spoke at once.

Jac, head and shoulders in the fridge as she rearranged dishes, giggled. "He's the rabbit who lives in the garden. Patricia named him Clarence."

Robert shook his head. "We seem to have a plethora of animals. Yes, the dogs did try to chase Clarence, but that wasn't the excitement. We met Donna and James Dayton and Thomas Cafferty in the garden."

"What on earth were they doing in the garden?" Shelbee asked.

I shook my head. "I don't know what Donna was doing there, but James and Cafferty were having an argument. James punched Cafferty, although he almost toppled over because he was drunk."

Shelbee replaced the lid on the cocoa tin. "Cafferty was drunk?"

"No," Robert said. "James was."

Jac popped her head over the fridge door. "He drank an awful lot of wine at dinner and took that bottle up to his room."

"What did they argue about?" Shelbee asked.

I shrugged. "I'm not sure. Cafferty said something odd, though. When Donna joined them, he told James that perhaps they should discuss Donna's criminal..." I turned to Robert. "What was the word?"

"Failings."

Jac closed the fridge door. "I wonder what he meant by that?"

I caressed Paw's ears. “I do too.”

Shelbee sipped her cocoa. “Okay, you two. Let it go.” She pointed to me. “I see your mind working furiously.” She pointed to Jac. “And don't encourage her. We have a mystery game to prepare for and no time to start chasing another mystery.”

Robert coughed into his hand. I suspected he was trying to stifle a laugh.

Jac saluted Shelbee. “Yes, sir. General, sir.”

We all burst into laughter as the dogs joined in barking and yipping.

I wiped tears from my eyes and shushed Paw. He stopped barking and fell against my side nearly toppling me. This was one of his demonstrations of love. But since he weighed close to two hundred pounds, he could physically push my short self around.

Robert rubbed Kathleen’s ears as Shelbee and Jac quieted Samuel and Bitsy. Kathleen jumped down from the counter to rub against Robert's legs, leaving Rascal to watch us with a bit of disdain.

I asked, “What more do we have to do in preparation for the game?”

Robert said, “You have to check out your costumes and Shelbee and I have to hide the murder weapons.”

“Murder weapons?”

“Yes. We've already distributed some clues to the participants. As they follow those clues, they will have the opportunity to find more clues and murder weapons.”

Shelbee enthused, “They're so cool. Hans Greble

carved them." She turned to me. "You know, the guy who sets up every week in the summer at the farmer's market."

I nodded.

"Hans has a small shop where he makes cabinets and other wood crafts. He offered to carve wooden representatives of murder weapons. A knife, a gun, a wrench, and a bottle."

She walked over to the kitchen counter, gave Rascal a pat, and unzipped her tote bag. She pulled out the wooden weapons.

Robert, Jac, and I walked over to join her, and she handed us each a weapon. I examined the gun. Its intricate detail was incredible. If not for the wooden texture of the object, it was easy to believe this was a real gun.

Robert held up the knife while Jac examined the bottle. From where I stood, the bottle was carved with a label on it. Poison.

We traded weapons back and forth.

"These are incredible," I said. "Hans is talented."

"He is," Shelbee said. "The idea was all Robert's though."

Robert blushed. "We use props in the theater. I thought it would add a bit of realism to the game."

Jac nudged him. "Plus, you love to play a detective."

Robert laughed. "Yes. Those are some of my favorite roles."

I handed the weapon I was holding, the knife, back to Shelbee. "I thought you were playing a police officer in the game."

"I am. A police inspector. But a bumbling one. The real detectives, who solve the case, are the players. I just bumble around creating confusion."

I nodded. "Who plays the dead man?"

"We have a dummy body prop from the theater. We plan to reveal the "deceased" tomorrow morning, then assemble everyone at breakfast and let them start the game."

I smiled. "I have a feeling some of them are already starting."

Robert looked at me with a quizzical expression.

"Donna asked if you would give any more clues outside, remember?"

He nodded.

"And based on my conversation at dinner with Ms. Wells, I'd say she is already on the case."

Robert sighed. "I'm glad they are eager to play, but I better hurry prepping tonight."

Shelbee placed the weapons back in her bag. "Then let's get started. Jac and I will hide the weapons while you finish preparations with the body."

Robert nodded.

I asked, "What can I do?"

Shelbee shook her head. "You go home and try on your costume. Be ready to get back here early tomorrow morning."

"I could stay the night."

"No. The inn is filled up, and I know Paw will sleep better at home."

Paw woofed.

Jac laughed. "See. He agrees."

I sighed. "Okay, but I've already tried my costume on half a dozen times. I know it fits."

"Do it again," Shelbee said.

Robert cuddled Kathleen to his chest. "Ladies, I'm going to take Kathleen up to our room. I'll see you all in the morning."

"Have a good night," I said as I gave Kathleen a scratch behind her ear.

"Meow."

Robert smiled and left the kitchen.

Jac walked to the door, stopping to give Paw and me a quick hug. "I'm going to do a quick check of the inn."

"Check the French doors. They were open earlier."

"Will do." Jac stepped through the kitchen door that connected to the dining room.

Shelbee walked over and hugged me.

"I'll walk you out."

I nodded, stepped to the kitchen counter to retrieve my bag, and gave Rascal a kiss. He head-butted my chin. I gave him one final kiss. "I'll see you tomorrow."

"Mreow."

Paw padded over. "Woof!"

Shelbee laughed at Paw's possessive bark.

"I love you too, jealous." I caressed his ears and then turned toward the door.

We strolled from the kitchen through the dining

room to the front door, Bitsy leading the way, tail curled over her back.

Paw plodded along beside me while Samuel followed, snuffling the floor for any stray bits of food.

Shelbee opened the door. Night had descended. "Are you sure you don't mind walking home alone? I could go with you."

"And walk back alone yourself? Don't be silly. This is Tranquil Valley."

"Yes, and you found a dead body in your neighbor's shed plus solved Robert's kidnapping. You find trouble."

I scowled. "I do not find trouble."

Shelbee huffed. "Fine. If you don't find trouble, then trouble finds you."

"Maybe, but you've been with me when trouble has shown up so how will you walking me home prevent trouble?"

"Hmm. Good point."

"Besides, I have Paw. He protects me."

Shelbee shook her head. "He finds more trouble than you."

"Woof!"

I laid my hand on his head. "You're a clever dog."

His tongue lolled out.

"All right," Shelbee said. "Get going. Call me when you get home, so I don't worry."

"I will." I gave her a hug and tugged on Paw's leash. After Paw and I stepped through the door and Shelbee closed it, I heard the lock click in place.

I pulled my flashlight from my bag but waited to click it on. A full moon bathed the area in a soft light, bright enough to see by. Paw pulled on the leash and trotted ahead.

The bed and breakfast sat on a hill to the south end of town. I walked down the front walkway and across the grass already damp from the night air. Paw reached the sidewalk and turned left.

From this vantage point, I could see across and into the main part of town. All appeared tranquil as its name implied. Cars lined the streets in places and lights shone from a few houses and local restaurants. Everything else was dark.

I switched on my flashlight and glanced at my watch. Eleven-thirty.

We walked down the hill at a brisk pace and turned left. An owl sailed overhead and Paw gazed up at it in interest.

"No. You can't chase him." I spoke to hear my own voice.

Goosebumps popped up on my arms as the night air chilled me. I'd left my jacket behind at the bed and breakfast.

Clouds scudded across the moon, so I switched on the flashlight. A comforting circle of light illuminated our path. Paw, whose eyes adjusted to low light, trotted ahead. Paw stopped now and then to sniff at something only his nose could sense. He stopped by a bush to mark his territory. Fortunately, the bush marked the beginning of the park where dog deposits of a liquid nature were accepted.

"Clarissa?"

I jumped at the voice behind me and whipped around, brandishing the flashlight as a weapon.

"Woof!" Paw's happy bark eased my mind.

CHAPTER 3

I shined the light on the face of the person in front of me.

Lillian Hardcastle, a petite seventy-year-old with snowy white hair, frowned at me. She raised her hand to shield her eyes. The light glinted off her glasses. "Lower your flashlight!"

"Sorry."

Paw pushed forward, trying to reach Lillian. I held tight to the leash, preventing him from jumping up on her. She reached out to pet Paw.

"What are you doing out so late, young lady?" Lillian was a close friend of my uncle, the police chief of our town. She'd known me all my life.

"Ms. Lillian, I could ask you the same thing."

"Hmph. You could, but I'm not answering until you tell me what you are doing walking alone out here."

I gestured to Paw who Lillian had continued to pet. He wore a blissful expression. "I'm not alone. I have Paw who is the best protection."

"Humph."

"Now why are you out here, Lillian?"

She shrugged. "I'm looking for Saber."

"Your cat?"

"Do you know any other Sabers?" She grumbled. "He's usually home by now."

I glanced at my watch. Five minutes to midnight.

I sighed, knowing Shelbee would be phoning if I didn't call her soon. Yet I couldn't leave Lillian to search for her cat alone.

"We'll help you search. Where does he usually hunt?"

"I don't need your help," she grumbled.

"Lillian, you and I both know that my uncle would have a fit if he knew I walked off and left you out here alone."

She nodded reluctantly. "He hunts all over, but the park is his favorite place."

I sighed with relief. We were standing on the edge of the park. At least we wouldn't have to walk all over town to look for Saber. I hoped.

"Your dog will scare him off."

I shook my head. No way was I going to walk Paw home and come back. "Paw won't scare Saber. I promise." I didn't add that Saber had the disposition of a cougar with a sore paw. Much like his owner.

She grumbled under her breath but started toward the park's interior calling, "Saber!"

I followed with Paw who trailed scents on the ground as I peered under bushes and up into trees.

Clouds scudded across the sky, intermittently obscuring the moon before its light burst forth to brighten the landscape. Bushes loomed in the darkness, and I tripped over dozens of tree roots. Lillian remained sure-footed as she tromped ahead calling her cat.

Paw woofed excitedly and barreled to a nearby tree. I shined the light up to reveal a squirrel sitting on a limb. It chattered at Paw who barked back.

"Now you decide to chase squirrels." I shook my head while he gazed up at the squirrel, growling softly.

The squirrel flipped his tail at us then scampered up the tree.

Paw barked once more before sniffing the base of the tree and trailing as I adjusted my hold on his leash. It would be just my luck that he would wrap his leash around the tree.

Lillian ignored us and bent down to look under one of the rhododendron bushes in the park. She stood up and called Saber. All I heard was the soft rustle of a light breeze and crickets chirping, but Paw raised his head.

He woofed and dragged me to a pear tree laden with fruit. He stood up, placing his paws on the tree trunk.

I heard a loud hiss amongst the tree branches.

"Saber?" Lillian hurried up to me, shoving me aside,

and searching the branches of the pear tree. "Saber, baby, is that you?"

"Mreow."

"Woof!"

"Hiss."

Lillian glared at Paw. "Hush, you, big galoot! You're scaring him."

"Lillian, he's trying to help."

"No, he's not. He's scaring my baby."

I tugged Paw down and back to my side. I knew there was no point in arguing with her, so I shined the flashlight into the tree branches.

Saber sat on a limb about midway up the tree. He turned his head as the light illuminated him to avoid the reflection off his eyes. His black fur coat absorbed the light. Saber was about six years old and had faced many battles, evidenced by his torn right ear and scar on his cheek. His disposition matched his owner's surly attitude.

Lillian pulled a bag of cat treats from her pocket. "Come on down, baby. Momma brought you your favorite treats. Yum! Yum!"

She turned to me. "Turn off that light!"

I switched off the flashlight and knelt to hold Paw, attempting to keep him quiet. I yawned. The sooner Lillian got her cat and I walked them home, the sooner I could get to bed.

Lillian rattled the bag, calling softly to Saber.

I heard a slight rustling and claws on bark. Paw whimpered, and I hushed him.

Lillian said, "Good boy, Saber. Here's your treat."

"Purr. Purr."

Paw shifted in my hold.

"Clarissa, turn on that flashlight. We need to get home. It's late."

I rolled my eyes before switching on the light.

Saber cuddled in Lillian's arms, purring and nuzzling Lillian's chin.

Paw pulled to get at the cat, but I held firm to him.

I pointed the light to illuminate our path as Lillian and Saber walked on my right with Paw on my left. Paw settled and ignored Saber who looked down at him with a smug expression.

Neither Lillian nor I spoke on our walk to her house. She lived on Curzon Street which was a small side street between the park and Main Street. We encountered no one on our walk home.

As we passed under one of the few streetlights, I saw a glint of light reflect off Saber's neck. I stopped.

Lillian continued a few paces then glanced back at me. "What?"

I motioned her back to me.

She tilted her head and stood with a frown on her face. I stepped up to her and pointed at Saber's neck where I now could identify the source of the light I'd glimpsed.

Saber wore a new collar. It appeared to resemble a metal bracelet with sparkling stones embedded in each metal link.

"That's a beautiful collar."

Lillian raised an eyebrow. "You okay, sugar? Feeling all right?"

I stared at her. "I'm fine, Lillian. Just admiring Saber's collar."

She shook her head. "Saber doesn't wear a collar."

"Well, he is now," I said, raising my flashlight to beam on Saber, who hissed and wriggled in Lillian's arms.

Paw whined at Saber. I caressed his ears to calm him before he further upset Saber.

"Easy, Saber, easy." Lillian's hand brushed his neck as she struggled to maintain a hold on the cat. "What?"

She caressed the cat's neck. "This isn't a collar." She worked at something amongst Saber's neck fur, and the item popped free.

A bracelet, the clasp flicked open, dangled from her hand. It glinted under the streetlight.

"Where did you get this, Saber?" Lillian nuzzled him.

Saber murped in reply, an innocent expression on his face.

Paw stretched forward and sniffed at the bracelet and Saber growled low in his throat.

I pushed Paw back, whispering for him to be good. The last thing we needed was for Saber to jump out of Lillian's arms and run away again. "We better get Saber home."

Lillian nodded as she stared at the bracelet. "Where could he have found this?"

We resumed our walk and turned right onto Curzon Street.

"I think the question is who put it on him."

"Saber won't let anyone but me touch him."

I sighed. "That's true, but this bracelet only closes with the clasp. I can't see Saber closing it around his neck."

Lillian frowned in thought.

We stepped onto her paved front path and climbed the porch steps. When Lillian opened her front door, Saber jumped out of her arms and sauntered in. She closed the door behind him and turned to me. "What should I do about this thing?" She held up the bracelet.

Momentarily speechless I stared at her. Lillian always knew what she wanted to do, never asking anyone's advice.

"Well?" She prompted.

I reached for the bracelet and examined it. "I don't see any identifying marks, but I would advise turning it in at the police station. Perhaps whoever lost it will check there for it. Of course, you could advertise it as found."

"Maybe." She chewed her lower lip.

"I wouldn't worry too much about it."

"Who says I'm worried?" she asked, hands on hips.

Paw woofed.

"Oh, hush, you, big galoot," Lillian said, but she caressed his ears and smiled at him.

"Good night, Lillian."

She nodded, opened the door to her house, stepped in, and shut the door.

Paw and I left the porch, strode down Curzon and turned onto Main Street. Within ten minutes, we were home.

The phone was ringing as I stepped through the door after Paw. I unhooked his leash, slammed the door shut, and hurried to the phone.

"Hello."

"It's about time." I imagined Shelbee standing with hand on hip, toe tapping, as she spoke. "Where were you?"

"Chasing a cat."

"Huh?"

I laughed. "Mrs. Hardcastle was out looking for Saber. I helped her find him."

"See, I told you trouble finds you." Shelbee's voice softened. "Was Saber all right?"

Shelbee loved animals and had a real talent for working with them. Her pet sitting business flourished.

"He was fine, except that he had a bracelet around his neck."

Shelbee gasped. "Was he choking? You did take it off, right?"

"Of course, and he's fine. It wasn't on too tight, but it is strange. How did he get a bracelet around his neck? There's no way he could have fastened it himself and Saber hates most people."

"That's true. Saber is his own cat. What did it look like?"

"Gold metal links with a clear-colored stone in each link."

"Valuable?"

I sighed and sat down on the floor, next to the table that held the phone. Paw lumbered up and plopped down next to me placing his head on my leg. "I have no idea."

"Hmm," Shelbee said. "I don't like it, but at least Saber is okay. I'll call Lillian in the morning and urge her to keep him indoors for his safety."

"Good luck with that."

"Yeah. See you in the morning. Bye."

"Bye." I hung up, placing the phone on the table by my head, and hugged Paw. "Shelbee thinks we find trouble."

He rolled his eyes up at me, innocent expression on his face.

The phone rang, and I jerked as the sound blared into my ear. Disturbed, Paw woofed.

Thinking it was Shelbee, I picked it up, saying, "I promise to try on the costume."

A deep male voice said with suggestive humor, "What kind of costume is it? A French maid's? An alluring vampiress?"

"You wish," I said to my boyfriend, Bruce Sever.

"A guy can dream."

"Mmmhm. So can a girl."

Bruce's hearty laugh boomed from the phone. "Why are you trying on a costume? Halloween is weeks away."

“It's for the murder mystery game at the B&B. Remember? I have a small role as a desk clerk.”

“Ah, you did tell me. Shame it's as a desk clerk. You'd look adorable as a maid.”

“Ha. Ha. How's your vacation?”

“Done. We cut our visit short because Tyler got called in.” Tyler worked as a security consultant. “The rest of the guys decided to go home.”

“Sorry to hear it. I know you were looking forward to seeing them.”

“We got some good fishing in and caught up on old times. I'm heading home and thought we could spend the weekend together, but I guess you're busy.” His voice held an edge of sadness.

Paw woofed into the phone.

Bruce spoke to him. “Hey, big guy, how you doing? Keeping her safe?”

Paw woofed and slobbered the phone in his delight to speak to Bruce.

I wiped the phone of drool with my sleeve and pushed Paw back.

“He's happy to hear that you're coming home.” I softened my voice. “As am I.”

“Can we spend time together?”

“Of course. My role is only a few lines early tomorrow; then I have the rest of the weekend free.”

“Great. I'll be home early this morning.” I glanced at the clock on the wall. It was past midnight, closing in on one.

"Why not come to the B&B and once I'm finished we can go out for lunch."

"Sounds good. See you soon. Love you." Paw woofed. "You too, Paw."

"I love you. See you."

I hung up the phone.

"Come on, boy. Let's go up to bed."

Paw jumped up, tail wagging, and headed to the stairs. I stopped to turn off the light sitting by the phone on the side table. A nightlight at the top of the stairs dimly lit my way as I dragged myself up the steps.

I yawned deeply.

By the time I reached the bedroom, Paw had jumped up onto the bed and was turning around in circles. I left him to his nightly ritual and crossed to the bathroom to brush my teeth.

I loved the old-fashioned bathroom with its claw foot tub. The house had been built a hundred years ago and required a never-ending list of repairs, but I cherished it. This house had been my grandmother's home all her life. When she passed away, I was shocked to discover that she had left the house to me. Fortunately, the house was paid off, and Jac's dad charged reasonable rates to fix whatever went wrong.

I replaced my toothbrush in its holder, changed into my nightgown, and switched off the light.

Paw stretched across the bed, eyes closed, waiting for me. He opened one eye as I sat on the edge of the bed.

"Move over." I nudged him.

He whimpered then rolled onto his back. I shook my head, figuring that was the most cooperation I would get from him.

I turned to the nightstand, glanced at the clock—1:00 am—and set the alarm. We needed to get up by 5:00. It was going to be a short night. I turned off the bedside lamp and crawled under the covers, falling asleep immediately.

My legs were pinned. I struggled to move while an incessant ringing sounded in my head. Everything was dark, and I felt both hot and cold.

"Woof!"

I jerked awake. The telephone was ringing by my bedside. I reached across, barely managing to lift the receiver. I looked down and discovered the source of my immobility. My two hundred plus pound Saint Bernard was laying across my lower body.

"Woof!" Paw said, staring at the phone.

As I dragged the phone to me, I hit the alarm clock, knocking it onto the floor with a thud.

"Hello." I pushed Paw off me.

Shelbee's tense voice whispered, "Cafferty's dead."

CHAPTER 4

"What?" I garbled as I rubbed my eyes to clear them of sleep.

Paw knew her voice too and had moved farther up the bed placing a heavy paw across my chest to snuffle the phone. I gave him a firm, but loving shove out of my face.

Trying to breathe from under a heavy paw, I glanced at the clock. Two in the morning.

"What's wrong?" I asked.

"I told you. Cafferty's dead. We need you here."

"How did he die?"

"He fell down the basement stairs."

My mind was beginning to wake up. "Why do you need me?"

"Because, silly, I don't think it's an accident."

I sat up, pushing Paw off me. "How do you know that?"

Shelbee raised her voice. "The murder mystery clue bottle is lying next to his body, and that bottle of wine William showed off at dinner is missing."

She lowered her voice. "I don't know what happened, but I've called the police. Your uncle will be here any minute. The thing is, Robert is worried that your uncle will accuse one of us since we were the last ones to handle the mystery bottle."

"Uncle wouldn't arrest anyone without probable cause."

"I know that, but Robert isn't the only one worried. William and your uncle Harry have had verbal fights at the last two town meetings. Patricia's afraid Harry will think William pushed Cafferty for stealing his wine."

"She's jumping to conclusions."

"Probably."

I yawned. "I'll be there in a few minutes."

I hung up the phone, climbed out of bed, and picked up the clock. 2:10 am. No wonder I felt so groggy. I dressed in jeans and a t-shirt, adding a sweater on top.

Paw led the way out of the bedroom and down the stairs. I grabbed my car keys, purse, and a jacket then walked out the door, locking it behind me.

Outside, Paw visited several bushes. How he could go again after the many times he had stopped on our way home mystified me. Once done, he trotted to the car's passenger side and woofed to get in.

Once we were both in the car, I started up, put the car in reverse, and started to back out, stopping at the sound of a siren. I waited as a police car with flashing lights flew past, then backed out onto the street and drove to the B and B.

"Woof!"

I pulled to the side of the road as a second police cruiser sped past me. No sirens, just lights flashing on this one.

I turned onto Curzon then left onto Park Lane. I slowed down as I reached the top of the hill where the B and B sat, lights blazing in every window. Police cars were parked askew in the inn's driveway with lights still flashing. I pulled up to the curb and stopped, put on the emergency brake, and turned off the engine.

Uncle Harry stood on the porch, hands on hips, staring at my car. He shook his head and motioned for me to join him.

I sighed and opened my door, holding it open for Paw to jump out, then retrieved my bag.

Paw bounded across the lawn and up the porch steps, slamming into Harry and wagging his tail.

Harry grabbed Paw's collar to keep my dog from slobbering his face. In a deep, gruff voice, he said, "Down, Paw! Yes. Yes. I love you too. Now, get down. Sit!"

Paw got down and sat.

I goggled at him. "He never obeys like that."

Harry pet Paw's back. "You don't use a commanding voice."

I shook my head, thinking Harry was wrong. Paw had

chosen to sit instead of obeying Harry's command, but I chose not to argue with my uncle.

Harry glared at me. “What are you doing here?”

“I'm here to help.”

“This is a police matter. I don't need a civilian's help.”

“Uncle, you know I've helped on previous cases.”

He grumbled under his breath. “More like interference.” Then said, “Go home.”

I crossed my arms. “I can't do that, Uncle. Shelbee called and asked me to come.”

“Shelbee isn't running this investigation. I am.”

My eyes widened as a woman stepped onto the porch from the front door.

Paw woofed and stood up, wagging his tail, then trotted over to greet her.

Harry ignored Paw and turned to his wife.

My aunt, Alma, never accompanied my uncle when he was on police work. She was in her early-fifties with light brown hair and merry brown eyes. Formerly Harry's secretary, Alma (nee May) resigned her position when she married Harry, citing conflict of interest.

Alma placed her hand on my uncle's arm. “Harry, dear, let Clarissa inside. I know her friends are eager to see her.”

Harry grumbled then nodded at me and jerked his head toward the door.

Alma bent and hugged Paw who wriggled at the loving attention. “How's my favorite Saint Bernard?”

Paw woofed and slurped her face.

From the corner of my eye, I glimpsed Harry smiling at their antics.

Alma straightened, turned, and led the way through the open front door, Paw following on her heels. As I stepped into the house, I saw several officers clustered on the left side of the central staircase talking amongst themselves. An open door, situated behind the staircase on the private kitchen side of the hall, stood open. The basement door, I guessed.

I heard a noise to my right and turned in time to brace for Samuel's joyous body slam. I staggered, and Harry grabbed my arm. I hadn't realized he had walked in behind me.

A chorus of woofs ensued as Samuel and Paw conversed.

Harry scowled at the ear-piercing welcome. "Quiet!"

Both dogs stopped barking, and the officers stopped conversing.

Shelbee walked into the ensuing silence from the living room on the right side of the foyer. She smiled at Uncle Harry, waved at Alma, and stopped next to me. "You got here fast."

Shelbee had the knack of calming any situation. It's one reason her pet sitting skills were sought out across the county.

She turned to Harry. "Shall I take Clarissa into the living room with everyone else?"

"Yeah. Do that. But no discussing the case until you give your statements. Same goes for the others."

Shelbee saluted which I was sure would anger Harry. Instead, he suppressed a grin, waved us away, and strode over to his men.

Alma hugged me. "See you later, sugar." She ruffled Paw's fur then joined Harry.

Shelbee and I led the dogs into the living room. An officer stood guard near the doorway to ensure we didn't speak to each other.

Besides Shelbee and me, everyone from the night before was in the room. Patricia huddled on the arm of an easy chair dressed in a purple robe. Her face looked haggard, and she leaned against William who shifted restlessly in the chair. William had pulled on jeans but still wore his pajama top of faded blue stripes. He scratched at his beard as he stared straight ahead, absently rubbing Patricia's arm.

Donna Dayton perched on the sofa beside her husband, James, who bent forward holding his head between his hands. James wore the same clothes I'd seen him in last night. His shirt was rumpled and hung askew on his shoulders as if he had slept in them. Donna wore a pair of black sweatpants and a blue tank top. I couldn't decide if she wore them for sleep or had thrown them on in a hurry.

Madeline Wells and Karen Taylor sat next to each other on the love seat. Madeline, who wore a flowered nightgown which peeked beneath a light blue robe, twisted her hands in her lap. She focused her attention on her hands. To my surprise, Karen Taylor was dressed to perfection in a deep blue pantsuit. Her hair was styled, and makeup applied, a sharp contrast to Madeline's disheveled hair and tear-streaked face.

Behind them, Robert paced back and forth. Every step he took, he ran a hand through his hair. He wore black pants and an untucked white shirt with a robe thrown on overtop.

The officer paid no attention to us as he stood statue-still and calm.

Someone was missing. I glanced around trying to determine who was missing besides Cafferty, of course.

Jessica. Cafferty's companion. Was she injured or killed? Shelbee had mentioned Cafferty's death. Could Jessica have been involved?

Plus, where was Jac? I thought she was staying the night at the inn. The cats, Kathleen and Rascal, plus Bitsy and Henry were missing too.

As I opened my mouth to ask Shelbee where they were, I heard a click and turned to find Jac opening the living room door with a tray of coffee clutched in her hands.

The officer held the door open and Jac smiled her thanks. She set the tray on the central coffee table. As she did so, the spoons and cups rattled.

"Stop that horrible noise! It's too loud!" James cried, clutching his head and rocking from side to side.

Donna shrugged and patted his back. To the room, she mouthed, "Sorry, hangover."

Robert, who had stilled at this outburst, resumed pacing.

Madeline was lost in her own thoughts, but Karen pinched her mouth in disgust.

Patricia stared in shock at James while William grimaced.

Jac filled cups with coffee, taking care not to make a sound. She handed the first cup to Patricia who grasped it in shaking hands. William shook his head in the negative when Jac offered him a cup.

Jac filled two more cups and handed them to Madeline and Karen.

Karen took the first cup and placed Madeline's hands around it, saying, "Drink. It'll help."

When Madeline didn't respond, Karen lifted Madeline's hands with the cup clutched in them and urged her to drink. Madeline took a few sips and Karen released her hands back to her lap. She accepted her own cup from Jac, nodded in thanks, and took a deep drink of coffee.

Jac turned to Donna and gestured to the coffee. Donna nodded then accepted the cup Jac poured. She forced one of James' hands from his head and thrust the cup into his palm.

James grunted and sniffed the coffee then jerked splashing coffee across himself and the floor as a loud bugling noise sounded from outside. "What the h—"

James didn't finish because another loud bugling cut him off. By now, William, Patricia, and the rest of the guests flocked to the windows to see the source of the noise.

"Woof! Woof!" Paw and Samuel added to the noise.

The police officer never moved, and Jac, Shelbee, and I shook our heads in amusement.

Shelbee sighed. "That sound is undignified for a man in his position."

I shrugged. "No one is ever going to change him."

The man in question was Hal McFarlane, my uncle's best friend and coroner for this area. Hal stood a little over five feet, but his diminutive stature belied a robust and energetic personality. Argumentative too.

He had a bugling horn installed in his late 1950s sedan and loved to use it. Uncle Harry considered him to be the best coroner he had ever worked with in his career. Conveniently, Hal lived in Tranquil Valley.

The bugling stopped and the shouting began.

Paw cocked his head, whining softly as he listened to the loud banter between Hal and Harry outside. Even inside, much of the conversation was easy to hear.

"What'd you get me out of bed for this time?" Hal's voice held a note of sleep to it.

Harry grumbled. "Since when do you sleep all night anyway?"

"That's my point. For once I was asleep until you called."

I patted Paw's back. He sighed and settled at my feet, head on paws.

Alma spoke in a voice so soft I missed some of her words. "Hal ---know---be here."

Hal laughed. "Even got your wife here. Good to see you, Alma." His voice boomed as they entered the house and stopped outside the living room doors.

"Where's the body?"

I noticed Madeline flinch at Hal's question.

Harry said in a curt voice, "This way."

As the men's voices moved away, the officer spoke. "Everyone should return to their seats."

William nodded and led Patricia over to the chair they had vacated. Robert refilled his cup of coffee as Karen led Madeline to the sofa. Donna urged James to his seat as Shelbee helped Jac wipe up the floor. James ignored the coffee soaking into his clothes in favor of holding his head in his hands again.

We sat in silence several moments before another set of raised voices broke the quiet.

A woman's nasally voice said, "I was not sneaking out. I needed to breathe."

A male voice spoke, "Ma'am. You can't be outside. We require all guests to stay in the living room."

"That's ridiculous. My boyfriend is dead, and you expect me to sit around with his murderer!"

CHAPTER 5

Everyone's head turned toward the doors. With a growl, James rushed to the door but was blocked by Officer Heldman.

Harry's voice rang through the house. "Who are you and who is murdered?"

Shelbee nudged me and I turned to face her. She mouthed, "Jessica."

I nodded.

Jessica's harsh voice answered, "As if you don't know. You're here, aren't you?"

Harry's voice hinted at exasperation. "We're investigating a death. No one said it was murder. Now who are you?"

"Jessica St. Clair."

"And who is...was your boyfriend?"

"Thomas Cafferty."

Harry grunted. "Then I have questions for you. Please go into the dining room and wait for me."

High-heels clicked across the floor then stopped. A door closed nearby.

I heard faint barking and Paw's ears stood up.

Heavy footsteps approached our room before the door flew open.

Harry stood in the doorway, scowling. "Shelbee, go with Officer Banks." He turned to Jac. "When she's done, you go next."

"Now wait a minute," James complained. "You can't keep us stuck here."

Harry glared at the man. "This is a police investigation. I advise you to cooperate. You'll get your turn to be questioned."

James paled.

Harry dismissed him from his attention and turned to me. "Clarissa, go into that kitchen and quiet those dogs. They're starving by the sound of it." The dogs increased their barking.

Shelbee stood up, handed Samuel's leash to me, and walked to the door. "They haven't been fed this morning."

"Feed them," he told me.

Patricia reminded me, "Give Henry his insulin when you feed him."

I stood, tightened my hold on the dogs' leashes and walked out. Paw trotted by my side, eager to see his friends.

I passed two of Hal's men carrying a stretcher. No

doubt for the body. As we passed the basement door, Hal emerged from it, stepping into the hall.

"There's my pretty girl," he said to me. Hal knew me since I was six years old. He always called me his pretty girl.

"Hi, Hal. Harry got you out of bed again?"

Hal laughed. "Yes. He did. Man's the bane of my life."

Some would find it callous that a man could laugh when someone had just died. But I knew Hal's emotions ran deep. He, like many of the other officers, was forced to face the most gruesome deaths on a regular basis. They developed a hard shell to do their jobs without going insane.

"You're best friends though."

"That we are." He shifted to let the men carrying the stretcher into the basement. This afforded me a view down the basement stairs. Steep, wooden steps descended with a wooden handrail on each side of enclosed steps. A bulb affixed to the ceiling cast the steps in bright light. A body lay face down, headfirst, at the bottom of the steps. The head appeared twisted at an awkward angle, facing left, the carved wine bottle on its side at his feet.

The dogs sniffed the floor around our feet and Paw tugged on his leash, eager to investigate the basement.

Hal stepped in front of the dogs and me. "You don't want to see that."

I stared into his eyes. "Was the fall the cause of his death?"

Hal never blinked. "You know I can't tell you that."

"Hit on the head?" I persisted.

Hal glanced back at his men descending the stairs. "Maybe."

I kissed his cheek and mouthed, "Thank you."

He blushed and waved me away with a pat on each dog's back.

I continued down the hall toward the private kitchen. The barking increased the closer I got, and Paw pulled at his leash to get to his friends.

I opened the door to wagging tails and jumping dogs.

Paw pushed through the crowd and stopped by the food bowls.

"You are one big stomach," I told him as I bent to pet Bitsy. Samuel slurped my face before greeting Bitsy while Henry woo-wooed a welcome.

"All right. Food's coming." I wiped my face of doggie kisses with a paper towel I found on the counter next to Rascal and Kathleen, who sat side by side with identical reserved expressions. Their look implied disdain at the dog's antics, but they too wanted breakfast.

Bags of dog food and cans of cat food were kept in a bottom cabinet. I bent to open the door. Rascal jumped on my back, walked to my head, and purred in my ear. Not so disdainful now.

I pulled out two cans of cat food and reached in for the huge bag of kibble. Rascal jumped off his rocking perch.

I dipped kibble into the dog bowls using a plastic cup.

The dogs pushed their heads in and began eating before I could finish dipping food. Ever thoughtful, Shelbee had left a bowl out for Paw as he was the first to start eating. I stuffed the bag back into the cabinet.

The cats paced the counter. I found a can opener in the top drawer above the dog food cabinet and opened the cans of cat food. Using a spoon from the same drawer, I divided cat food into two bowls. Rascal pushed in before I was finished, but Kathleen sat with tail wrapped around her body. She was a lady. I placed her bowl in front of her, and she ate dainty bites. Rascal finished first and stretched a paw toward her bowl. With one quick flash, Kathleen smacked at him, and Rascal withdrew. A lady had her limits after all.

Henry needed his insulin shot since he was eating. Shelbee had taught me how to give insulin and Patricia had instructions on dosage posted on the fridge. I took out the insulin vial and a syringe. I prepped the syringe but discovered the insulin level in the vial was too low. I searched the fridge for a new one but didn't find another vial. Perhaps one was in the commercial fridge. I left the animals eating and crossed the hall to search the fridge in the commercial kitchen. Success.

"I will not." A voice spoke from behind me making me jump. I spun around to confront the person but discovered no one was there. Was the person hiding?

A muffled but familiar grumble drifted from behind the connecting door to the dining room. Of course. Harry was interviewing Jessica.

I padded over to the door. Could I hear their conversation through the door? I placed my ear against the door and heard some clear words interspersed with periods of conversation too low to understand.

Harry coughed. "Why did...Cafferty...inn?"

Jessica's response was garbled as well. "...getaway...murder mystery."

The conversation continued, but I gleaned nothing more. I tiptoed from the door although I doubted they could hear me in the dining room. I crossed to the private kitchen where I prepped Henry's insulin. Henry docilely sat for his injection. I disposed of the syringe and empty insulin vial and put the new vial in the fridge.

I emptied and refilled the water bowls for both the dogs and the cats. By the time I finished with the water, every bit of food had been devoured.

A voice behind me made me jump. "They'll need a walk."

I turned to see Shelbee standing in the kitchen doorway. She held three leashes in her hand.

"I didn't hear you."

She smiled. "You were too busy murmuring and cooing to the them." She nodded to the animals.

I put my hands on my hips in mock outrage. "I do not murmur or coo."

Shelbee closed the kitchen door and walked over to Samuel.

I gestured to the cats. "Do they need their kitty pans cleaned?"

Shelbee clicked on Samuel's leash. "Yes, but it can wait until after we walk the dogs."

I took a leash and snapped it on Henry.

Shelbee snapped the final leash on Bitsy who danced in place.

I retrieved Paw's leash from the floor, and he led the way to the kitchen door connecting to the back garden.

Paw trotted outside as soon as I opened the door. Henry stopped to sniff the doormat, and I was stretched between the two dogs. Shelbee solved the problem by giving Henry a gentle nudge.

The basset wooed and plodded forward. Samuel and Bitsy followed as Shelbee shut the door.

She let the dogs lead us where they chose. "Learn anything?"

"Now what makes you think I learned something?"

Shelbee laughed. "Come on. I know you, remember? You can't resist a mystery. That's why I called and asked you to come over here."

I shrugged. "True, but you could have waited until morning."

Shelbee shook her head. "Robert was worried because our clue wine bottle was found with the body."

My eyes widened. "You saw the body?"

"Yes. Did you?"

"I got a quick look when I stopped to talk to Hal. How did you see the body?"

She sighed. "I think we all saw it. At least, the guests, Robert, Jac, and I plus Patricia and William."

She stood a moment staring into space. The dogs sniffed the grass around a bench in the garden. "Odd. I don't think Jessica was there."

"Why is that odd?"

"Two reasons. She and Cafferty shared a room, and Madeline Wells screamed so loud no one could sleep through that noise."

I was confused. "Maybe you better tell me everything that happened after I left."

"Okay." Shelbee took a moment to organize her thoughts. "After you left I hid the weapons and clues. I checked with Robert and Jac that they were finished then Jac and I went up to our room. Since the inn was full, Patricia arranged for us to share their second bedroom on the third floor. That's where their personal rooms are located. I didn't hear or see anyone including Patricia or William. Jac and I got ready for bed, and I fell asleep as soon as my head hit the pillow.

"The dogs roused me a couple of times, whining and restless. I shushed them and went back to sleep. Later I woke to loud screams and the dogs howling. Jac and I stared at each other in confusion then grabbed our robes and rushed out of our room. The dogs pushed out too. Patricia joined us on the landing while Henry trotted ahead to William, who was already at the bottom of the third-floor stairs.

"We ran down the stairs and met Karen Taylor coming out of her room. Donna Dayton flung open her door and joined us. We descended to the first floor where lights were blazing. I assumed William turned them on. We turned toward the basement."

I opened my mouth to ask a question, but Shelbee anticipated it. "The woman screamed again. That's how we knew where to go. Once in the hallway, I saw Madeline Wells rocking back and forth on her feet, standing in the center of the hallway. The basement door was open, and light shone out.

"Karen pushed by me and ran to Madeline. She embraced her and mumbled words I couldn't hear.

"The rest of us hurried down the hall and looked through the door. William was hunched over the body, checking for a pulse. I went down the stairs to help William while Jac stayed with Patricia.

"Donna Dayton said, 'Is he dead?' And William nodded.

"I observed the body and surroundings and was considering what to do when Madeline started yelling, 'murder.' Karen tried to calm her, but she was hysterical. Patricia and Jac went to help Karen and William asked me to call the police."

Paw pushed his head and shoulders under a bush as he trailed a scent. Samuel lay down at Shelbee's feet while Henry rolled on his back. Bitsy stood up against Shelbee's leg, begging to be held.

Shelbee lifted her for a cuddle as I asked, "Where were Robert and James?"

Shelbee shrugged. "I don't know about James, but

when I left the basement, Robert stood at the top of the steps. You don't suspect Robert, do you?"

I sighed. "No, but I want to know where everyone was when Cafferty was found."

Henry rolled up to standing and stared at something behind us. "Woo. Woo."

Jac strolled across the grass to us. "Discussing the case?"

"Yes," I said, as Paw wiggled out from under the bush. "I guess you've been questioned."

"Officer Banks asked me a few things as a formality."

Shelbee adjusted Bitsy in her arms. "Did you see Jessica?"

"No, but I heard her. She yelled as she left Harry that 'he better find out who killed Thomas.' Then she stomped up the stairs to the guest rooms. Harry came out of the dining room scowling and called James Dayton into the room."

"Uncle will solve the case."

Shelbee set a wiggling Bitsy on the grass. The dog scampered over and found a convenient bush to do her business. Shelbee watched her a moment then said, "Clarissa asked me about last night, Jac. Why don't you tell her what you remember?"

"Sure." Jac recited her version of last night's events which mirrored what Shelbee told me. "Patricia escorted Donna into the living room and asked me to pen the dogs in the kitchen. We sat on the sofa and tried to calm her. James stumbled in and demanded to know what was happening. I asked him where he'd been, and he claimed he was in bed. Donna glared at him."

"Sounds to me like James was lying." I extended my arm to allow Paw to walk around a tree.

Jac shrugged. "I think Karen Taylor was lying as well."

Shelbee cocked her head on the side. "Why do you say that?"

"Didn't you notice? She was wearing her full make-up. Wouldn't she have cleaned it off before bed?"

Shelbee shrugged. "Maybe she was too tired."

I walked around the tree to unwrap Paw's leash. "Let's walk."

All four dogs waved their tails as we strolled through the garden.

Jac scratched Samuel's ears as she said to me, "Did you talk with Hal?"

"Yes. He couldn't confirm anything but admitted it was possible Cafferty could have been hit on the head."

"I think he was," Shelbee said. "I saw blood in his hair."

"He could have hit his head as he fell," Jac pointed out.

Paw woofed. He'd caught a scent as did Henry who, tail in the air and nose to the ground, tracked the scent.

I ran to keep up with them as they led me to the back of the garden. They stopped and circled a huge mulch pile.

"Woo-woo!" Henry barked at Paw who woofed back then began to dig. Mulch flew in all directions. Shelbee, Jac, and I were hit with bits of bark. Bitsy hid behind Shelbee's legs, but Samuel pushed in to help Paw dig.

I tugged hard on Paw's leash, but he was determined to dig. Jac reached forward and pulled on Paw's collar as Shelbee grabbed Samuel's. Henry sat back and watched.

Together we pulled the dogs back. Jac, who was closest to the hole, said, "He found something."

CHAPTER 6

I sighed. "He usually does. What is it this time? A dead mouse."

"No. A wine bottle."

"What?" Shelbee and I exclaimed.

Jac nodded at the hole. "See for yourself."

Shelbee leaned forward and shook her head. "She's right."

I glanced down at Paw who sat staring up at me with a smug smile on his face. His tongue lolled out and he brushed his tail back and forth on the grass behind him.

I looked in the hole then at Paw. "Sorry, boy. I didn't mean to doubt you. You've done it again. Found another clue."

We took the dogs back inside, and I went to find Harry. He was escorting Donna Dayton from the dining room. "Thank you, Mrs. Dayton, for your cooperation."

She nodded, crossed the foyer, and climbed the stairs to the upper floors.

"Uncle, I need to tell you something."

Harry motioned for me to follow him into the dining room. "What is it?"

"The girls and I took the dogs outside for a walk."

Harry perused his notes as he half-listened to me.

"I think Paw found a clue."

Harry's gaze shot up at me. "Show me."

I led the way back outside to the back of the garden and the mulch pile. I pointed at the hole Paw dug.

Harry stepped closer to the mulch and peered into the hole. "You touch anything?"

"No, sir."

"Good. Stay here a minute."

He strode back to the house and returned within a minute with one of his officers and a tech guy. "Bag it," he said to the tech. To the officer, he said, "Search the area."

"Yes, sir."

Harry took my arm and led me back to the house. We entered the private kitchen where Shelbee and Jac waited with the dogs.

"Woof!" Paw rushed to Harry as the other dogs began to bark.

Shelbee and Jac shushed the others as Harry pet Paw. "Good work, Paw."

The dog lapped up the attention.

Harry sat down at the kitchen table. "Tell me how you found the bottle."

I recounted how Paw and Henry trailed a scent to the mulch.

Harry shook his head. "Wouldn't the odor from the mulch throw the scent off?"

"I would think so, but somehow Paw and Henry knew it was there."

"Or got lucky." Harry scribbled notes.

"Either way, that's the bottle of wine William showed us at dinner last night."

Harry grunted. "You sure about that?"

"That bottle is identical to the one William displayed at dinner last night. Why would anyone leave it in a mulch pile unless they were hiding it?"

Harry grunted.

"According to Cafferty and Donna Dayton, that wine is expensive and highly-rated. I doubt a second bottle of wine would be at the inn. Last night, William left the table saying he would return it to the wine cellar. How did it get in the mulch pile?"

Harry set down his pen. "I'll speak with William next."

"What do you want me to do?"

"Go home." Harry stood up. "You stay out of this case, Clarissa."

I opened my mouth to protest, but Harry spoke before I could say anything. "I mean it. Go home."

I sighed, knowing he wouldn't relent no matter how much I argued. "I need to tell Shelbee I'm leaving."

Harry nodded and motioned for me to go.

I left the kitchen and walked across the hall to the

commercial kitchen. As I stepped through the door, I heard Patricia say, "This is terrible. I don't know what to do. Are the guests going to stay or leave?"

Harry, who had followed me into the hall, stepped in behind me. "I have informed your guests that I will have more questions, but I can't force them to stay in town. It would help my investigation if you can convince them to stay."

"We'll try." Patricia dusted off her hands. She placed dough into a baking pan and opened the oven door.

Harry turned and left the room.

Patricia took off her apron. "How are we going to convince them to stay?"

Shelbee sliced strawberries. "Continuing the murder mystery game seems in poor taste. Any ideas?"

Jac and Patricia stood thinking in silence.

"Will you need me?" I asked as I picked up a strawberry to eat. My stomach growled.

"Are you hungry again?" Shelbee walked to the fridge and opened the door. She pulled out a carton of eggs. "I'll make you some breakfast."

Patricia lifted down a skillet hanging over the central work island. "Good idea. Let's put out a buffet breakfast for the guests and ask them what they would like to do this weekend."

I took over Shelbee's job of slicing strawberries while she cooked eggs as Jac and Patricia prepared toast and bacon.

William stepped into the kitchen, running a shaking hand through his hair. "What can I do?"

Patricia adjusted the temperature on the stove. "Go to the shed and bring in two of the folding tables. Set them up in here."

"Why?"

"Because the police are using the dining room."

William saluted her and left.

"Clarissa, make a fruit salad." Patricia opened the fridge. "We have blueberries, melons, peaches, pears, and apples to add to the strawberries you're cutting."

Shelbee placed a plate of eggs in front of me. "Here eat this first. Don't want you dying of starvation."

Patricia and Jac paused in their preparations.

"Oops." Shelbee grimaced. "Sorry. Wrong choice of words."

Patricia smiled weakly and closed the fridge door. She went back to frying bacon.

Jac nudged Shelb's shoulder. "No worries."

I gulped down the eggs. They were delicious. I rinsed my plate and fork then placed them in the dishwasher before opening the fridge. Shelves upon shelves of a variety of foods filled the space. This was the largest refrigerator I had ever seen, designed specifically for a commercial kitchen.

I grabbed several melons and closed the door then set them on the central island. Using a butcher knife, I cut a cantaloupe in half then cleaned out the seeds.

Jac handed me a melon baller and a glass dish.

As I scooped small, round balls of melon, I said, “Patricia, what do you know about Thomas Cafferty?”

“Not much, I'm sorry to say. He reserved a room two days ago. When he arrived, he paid in cash. He never told us that he was bringing someone with him.”

Jac removed toast from the multi-slice toaster. “I thought the rooms had been booked months in advance because of the murder mystery game.”

“They had been.” Patricia lifted strips of bacon out of the pan and onto a serving dish. “Every guest here is a last-minute arrival since we had to cancel the original bookings when the roof leaked. The Daytons were the only ones who agreed to change dates. The others booked within the last two weeks. Cafferty booked a room but never mentioned he was bringing Jessica.”

I finished the cantaloupe and cut open a honeydew. “What did you do?”

“I told him he would have to pay for her room. He waved that away, saying they would share a room. I told him he would have to pay for her as well. He ordered - can you believe it – ordered me to get my husband for him to speak with. I told him that I ran this B&B and he would deal with me.”

She shook her head. “He paid her share but insisted on the bridal suite. I relented and let him have it since the honeymoon couple from Arizona canceled at the last minute.” She grumbled, “Should have charged him more for the room.”

Shelbee snorted. “He was a real jerk.”

William carried in two tables and unfolded them, setting them up to one side of the room. "What's next?"

Patricia walked over and wiped the tables with a damp cloth. She gestured to a closed door. "Tablecloths."

William opened the door, revealing shelves of linens and supplies.

"William," I asked as I scooped out honeydew, "what did you think of Cafferty?"

I noticed William's shoulder muscles tense. "Cafferty? He was a rude jerk." He glanced at me. "I probably shouldn't say that with his recent death, but he was."

Jac finished stacking toast and put her hands on her hips. "I wonder what he was doing near the basement so late at night?"

I squinted at her. "What do you mean?"

"Why go to the basement in the middle of the night? What's down there? Or did someone lure him there?"

"You mean to kill him?" Shelbee asked.

Jac shrugged.

I nodded. "According to Hal, Cafferty could have been hit on the head. He'll know more after the autopsy."

"Who is Hal?" William glanced at Patricia as he picked out two tablecloths. "Have I missed something?"

She shrugged. "If you did, so did I."

I set down the melon baller. "Hal is the county coroner. I've known him for ages."

Jac persisted. "So why was Cafferty in the hall by the basement in the middle of the night?"

Shelbee turned off the stove. "For that matter why was Madeline Wells in the hall?"

"And how long did Cafferty lie there before she found him?" Jac looked to me. "Did Hal know the time of death?"

"He didn't mention it, but we didn't have long to talk."

William cleared his throat. "I don't know about Madeline, but my guess is Cafferty wanted to search the wine in the basement."

"Really?" Shelbee scraped the last eggs out of the pan and onto a plate. "He was disdainful of the wine you served at dinner."

"True," William said. "But he was interested in the Chateau Haut Brion, and he knew that I returned it to the basement."

"He wasn't the only one interested in that wine," Patricia pointed out as she and William draped the tablecloths over the tables. "Donna Dayton knew the value of it."

Jac said, "I'm surprised Mr. Dayton didn't know."

"Maybe he did," I said, "but was too drunk to remark on it. What I wonder is who stole the wine from the basement and why leave it in the mulch?"

Patricia shifted nervously while William shrugged. He said, "The mulch pile is a terrible place to hide wine. Too hot and humid. Whoever stole it, if it was stolen, doesn't know wine."

"Or needed to hide it quickly," Jac said.

Patricia waved away our conversation. "Best get this food served. I wonder how long the police will be here?"

I finished arranging the bowl of fruit salad. "Hard to say. Sounds like Harry is still interviewing." I could hear a murmur of indistinguishable voices through the closed passthrough door.

William grunted. Patricia observed his expression. "Didn't it go well?"

I assumed she referred to his questioning.

William shrugged. "Could've gone better." He glanced at the rest of us then turned back to his wife. "We'll talk later."

Rats. I was hoping to learn what Harry and William had discussed.

Jac picked up a plate of toast. "Who's going to inform the guests?"

"I'll do it," William answered as he strode to the door to the hall.

Shelbee nudged me. "What about Harry and his officers?"

"We'll take them coffee and pastries. That way the guests can eat in peace."

Jac sat a carafe of orange juice on one of the folding tables. "You two take food to the officers. I'll stay here and help Patricia serve the guests as they arrive." She winked at us which meant she'd listen to the guests and gently question them.

"Hmm," Shelbee said. "Some of the officers and techs are gathering evidence around the mulch pile." She gazed at me with a quirked eyebrow. “Why don’t we offer them some coffee? Maybe learn something?”

I smiled broadly. “Good idea.”

Shelbee grabbed a carafe of coffee and paper cups while I carried a tray of the same pastries Jac had offered the guests earlier. It felt like ages ago but was only a few hours.

I motioned with my chin to the backyard. Shelbee nodded, but instead of crossing the hall to the private kitchen and its back door, she hung a right.

“Harry won't want us to interrupt the basement crime scene,” I warned as I balanced the tray.

“Not my plan.”

“Then where are we going?”

Shelbee maneuvered past the officers by the basement door, cut across the foyer, and to the living room. Karen Taylor passed us in the doorway with Officer Banks following her. In the living room, James Dayton sat hunched in the same position as earlier. Officer Heldman stood guard.

Shelbee nodded ahead. “Through the French doors.”

The French doors opened onto the side of the house, facing the parking lot. “Why this way? The private kitchen and back door are closer.”

She rolled her eyes. “And the dogs would knock you over and eat those pastries in a minute.”

My mouth formed an “O.”

We stepped out onto the stone patio, closed the door firmly behind us, and turned the corner of the house. I gazed across the lawn to the three police officers who were combing the area around the mulch pile. All wore latex gloves.

Shelbee led the way, waving to the officers as we approached. “Would you guys like some coffee?”

Rob Barnes, one of Harry's deputies, waved back. “Sure would.”

The other two officers peered over their shoulders at us. They both wore jackets emblazoned with “Dockers PD” on them. Harry must have the neighboring sheriff for support.

Rob motioned to us. “They're okay. Clarissa,” he indicated me with a wave of his hand, “is the Chief's niece.”

Both men nodded and stood to accept a cup of coffee from Shelbee. One took a pastry from my tray while the other declined. Rob grabbed a cruller and gulped the coffee Shelbee handed him.

I smiled and handed him a napkin. “How's the investigation going?”

The other two men lowered their brows, no doubt prepared to tell me that was confidential. Rob had no such concerns.

“Early days yet,” he said. “We'll soon be finished here, and when they get done questioning, we'll clear out.”

“Find anything more?” I motioned to the mulch.

“Only what you found.”

One of the officers cleared his throat. Rob glanced at him and shrugged. “She's solved murder cases before.”

The officer raised an eyebrow then went back to sipping his coffee.

Rob turned back to me. "But that's all I'm telling you. Chief doesn't want you involved, you know."

I sighed. "I know."

Before I could wheedle any more information out of Rob, Officer Heldman strode toward us.

Shelbee, who had been conversing with the other Docker's officer, held up the coffee carafe. "Want some?"

Heldman nodded and hurried over. Shelbee poured him a cup. He took a long drink then smacked his lips. "That's good coffee."

"Harry done with the interviews?" I asked as I held the tray out to him.

Officer Heldman, Steven to his friends, replied "almost" as he took a Danish. "Banks is finishing with the Taylor woman, and Harry is questioning James Dayton."

Rob finished his cruller. "I better gather up our equipment because the Chief will want to leave when he's finished." He strode off toward the house.

Both Docker's officers finished their evidence gathering and strode after him.

I turned to Heldman and opened my mouth to speak, but he interrupted me. "I won't answer your questions." He shook his head. "Rob talks too much."

I pursed my lips in frustration.

Heldman nodded to the house. "He said he told you to go home. I advise you to get your dog and do it." Then he strode back to the house.

"Humph," Shelbee said next to me. "He's no help."

I shrugged. "Not surprising."

As Heldman went to walk through the French doors, he paused. Jac stepped out and smiled at Heldman. He nodded then went inside.

Jac strode over to us. "Any luck?"

"No," I said then paused to listen.

"Woof."

I recognized that bark.

Shelbee turned to face the back of the B&B. "They're restless. They can sense the tension emanating from the guests."

Henry joined Paw, wooing his displeasure. Answering barks came from Bitsy and Samuel.

"Let's get them into the garden again." I strolled to the back door.

Shelbee and Jac followed me, Jac saying, "Most of the guests have left."

"What?" Shelbee stopped and stared at her. "The Chief wants them to stay in town."

"They didn't leave town, just the B&B. They didn't check out either. I don't know where James or Donna Dayton is. Neither came for breakfast."

I said, "Heldman said Harry was questioning James Dayton."

"Jessica grabbed toast and swore she was going to find somewhere else to stay," Jac added.

I turned the doorknob, and Samuel and Bitsy rushed out to Shelbee. Bitsy stood up against Shelbee's leg while Samuel pushed his nose against her side.

Paw pushed through next, and I gave him a big hug. "Sorry, boy. I promise to spend more time with you."

"Woof." He licked my cheek, coating me in doggie drool.

Henry scooted past us, woo-wooing in delight at newfound freedom. I grabbed a towel, to wipe my face and the dogs' leashes.

Jac was bent over talking to Henry when I got outside. "Hey, sweetheart. How are you?"

Henry's tail was wagging a mile-a-minute.

I snapped on Paw's leash and handed Henry's to Jac. "Did anyone else leave?"

Shelbee pulled leashes from her pocket and attached them to her dogs' collars.

Jac stood up. "Yes. Karen Taylor made an egg sandwich and announced she "had to get out of this madhouse." I watched her leave through the front door. Madeline Wells shrugged at her friend's dramatics, finished her breakfast, and climbed the stairs to her room. But Robert left to check on Pedro."

Pedro was Robert Roberts' pet parrot. He was a talkative bird that had helped on a previous case.

Samuel pulled at his leash, sniffing the grass. Shelbee let him take the lead. She looked at Jac. "Did you learn anything from the guests during breakfast?"

"No. All Ms. Wells wanted to talk about was the

murder mystery game. I think she thinks we're going to continue with it."

I stopped as Paw sniffed around a garden bench. Patricia had placed several throughout the garden for guests to rest. "Why would she want to continue the game? She was shaking this morning from the discovery of the body."

"I don't know why, but she sounded passionate about the game. She kept asking when it would begin. I think that's one of the reasons Robert left. He didn't even stop to find Kathleen."

Shelbee, pet-sitting professional that she was, asked, "Where is Kathleen?"

Jac adjusted Henry's leash. "Patricia put both cats in her apartment."

Shelbee's shoulders relaxed. "Good. They'll be happier there." She paused a moment in thought. "Maybe we should go on with the game."

"Why?" I asked as I untangled Paw's leash. Somehow, he always managed to wrap it around objects. In this case, the bench.

"If we continue with the game, it will keep the guests here as your uncle wants. Perhaps the killer will slip up and reveal his, or her, self. And we can use the game to question them." She shook her head. "Of course, that could be dangerous if the killer figures out what we're doing."

"If Cafferty's death was murder," I reminded her, "Hal didn't confirm it was murder."

"True," Shelbee said, "but he didn't deny it either. And someone moved the wine bottle to the mulch pile. It's too coincidental that the wine went missing at the same time Cafferty died if you ask me."

I freed the leash from around the bench. "It's worth a try as long as we are careful. Robert will have to agree since he plays the key role in the game, but I think the actors from the theater who were going to take part should be kept out of it."

Henry rolled over, scratching his back in the grass. Jac rubbed his belly. "But we need one more person to fill out the roles."

Paw leaped to his feet and lunged, stretching the leash to its full extent. "Woof!"

Samuel, Bitsy, and Henry all stood and barked as well.

I dug in my heels to hold on to Paw and glanced in the direction he was looking, then grinned. "I found our replacement actor."

CHAPTER 7

Shelbee and Jac turned to look in the direction I was staring. Shelbee rolled her eyes while Jac laughed, saying, "If you can get him to do it."

Bruce Sever strode toward us, his long legs crossing the distance with ease. He winked at me and patted Paw on his shoulder. "My two favorites."

"Hey," Shelbee teased, "what about Jac and me?"

"And the dogs," Jac added pointing to our canine companions.

Bruce crossed his arms and studied them. "Well..."

Shelbee playfully slapped his arm and turned to Jac. "I get the impression we're not wanted. Let's go inside and let the lovebirds have a moment."

Jac giggled and followed Shelbee and the dogs into the house.

I urged Paw to sit then hugged Bruce. “This is a surprise.”

“We were to meet this morning. When I went to your house and didn't find you, I thought I'd try here. You are playing in the mystery game, right?” He turned to look back at the house. “You didn't tell me Harry was participating. Those police cars add a realistic touch.”

I sighed, knowing Bruce would have a fit when he found out that I was involved in another murder investigation. “They aren't part of the play. One of the guests died.”

He whipped his head back around to me. “How?”

“Fell down the basement stairs.”

Bruce groaned. “Don't tell me. You're involved in another murder.”

I put my hands on my hips. “I resent your tone, Bruce. I can't help it if people die.”

“But you can stay out of the investigation.”

I glared at him. “Would you?”

He grunted.

“I could use your help.”

Bruce just stared at me without answering.

Paw stood and head-butted Bruce's leg.

“You want me to help her, don't you, boy?” He ruffled Paw's fur.

“Woof!”

“Yes. We have to take care of our best girl.”

Paw wagged his tail.

I stayed silent, biting back a retort that I could take

care of myself. "Good. You can have a part in the mystery game."

Bruce raised one eyebrow. "Game?"

"The murder mystery game that we planned. Shelbee, Jac, and I are going to suggest the game be played." I raised a hand, palm out, when Bruce opened his mouth to speak. "I know it seems in poor taste with Cafferty's death, but one of the guests has been asking if the game will continue. The girls and I think that playing the game may reveal a killer."

"Cafferty?"

"Thomas Cafferty. He's the guest who fell down the basement steps. Hal thinks the guy may have been hit on the head causing his fall."

Bruce scowled. "What aren't you telling me?"

"One of the weapons from the game was found by the body."

"Weapons!"

"Carved wooden replicas of a knife, a gun, a bottle, and a wrench. I saw the bottle lying at the dead man's feet."

Bruce crossed his arms. "You saw the body?"

"Just a glimpse." I glanced at the mulch pile. "And a bottle of wine William showed us last night at dinner is missing. Paw found it in the mulch." I nodded to behind me.

"Woof!"

Bruce smirked at Paw. "Of course, he found it."

Bruce scratched his jaw. "Continuing the game could be dangerous. The killer may strike again."

"I know, but we don't know if there is a killer. Harry wants to keep the guests busy while he investigates."

"You plan to investigate too."

I nodded. "And I'd like your help."

Bruce turned and stared at the house. A frown marred his face indicating he was deep in thought. He turned back to me. "All right. We'll do this. But," he pointed a finger at me, "you won't take any risks. If you even suspect who the murderer is, you tell me. No confrontations."

I refrained from rolling my eyes. I could have reminded him that I never intentionally confronted a criminal, but Bruce would have listed off all the times I had been in danger.

Instead, I hugged him, saying, "Thank you."

Paw wedged himself between us with a "woof!"

Bruce gave me a quick kiss on the cheek and took Paw's leash. Under his breath, I heard him say, "I'm going to regret this."

I let it go, and we walked back to the B&B.

We crossed through the back door, out the kitchen, and into the foyer. I didn't see Harry or his police officers.

Bruce and I needed to find Shelbee and Jac to plan how we would use the mystery game to draw out a possible killer. That is if the rest of the guests were willing to participate. Plus, we needed to get Patricia and

William's okay. Perhaps they wouldn't feel it appropriate to conduct the game after Cafferty's death.

From the foyer, I heard Patricia and William's raised voices in the living room.

"William, that was a stupid thing to do. You should have told him the truth."

"And risk being accused of Cafferty's death? No way!"

Bruce glanced at me, placing a finger to his lips. Together we edged closer to the foyer.

Patricia cursed.

I was so shocked I stopped walking. Patricia was the one person I knew who remained calm and serene.

"Easy, Patty. It will be okay. We didn't kill the guy."

"But what if the Chief thinks otherwise."

"Then I'll convince him."

I heard William's heavier footsteps heading toward the door.

Before we could move, William bolted out the living room door then stopped when he saw us. He glared at Bruce. "You a cop?"

Bruce stretched up to his full height. "No, but I am a private detective, and I think you should explain the conversation we just heard."

"That's none of your business."

"It is my business," Bruce said, "if a crime was committed."

Patricia rushed out to defend William. "He didn't commit any crime."

Paw turned his head, glancing at each of us. He shifted, restless, as he sensed the tension amongst us.

I stroked his head to soothe him and he licked my hand. I addressed William. "But you are afraid of being accused of murder."

Patricia answered. "We're all afraid of it. Cafferty was a wicked man."

"Patty," William warned in a growl.

Bruce took a different approach. "Do you have an alibi for the time of death?"

"We were together." William hugged Patricia.

"How do you know what time he died?" I only had a guesstimate based on Hal's observations.

"We don't," Patricia said, "but from the time you left until Madeline screamed, we were in our apartment. Jac can attest to the fact that both William and I left our room to meet her in the hallway when we heard the scream."

"You could have slipped out sometime in between." Bruce's face was stony.

"Then you'll have to take our word for it." William glared back at Bruce. "Now, if you'll excuse us, we have work to do."

Together they stepped around us and walked toward the kitchen areas.

"Do you believe them?" I looked down at Paw who was sniffing the foyer floor. No one was around, so I unhooked his leash. He followed a scent trail to the stairs.

"No. Do you?"

I sighed. "I want to. They've been wonderful to Jac and the rest of us. I hate to think one of them is a murderer."

"Or both," Bruce added.

Paw stood staring up the stairs.

"What motive would they have for killing Cafferty?"

Bruce shrugged. "That's something we'll have to find out."

Paw started up the steps.

"Paw. No." I ran to catch him, but he put on a burst of speed.

"Come back here, Paw!"

He ignored me. He reached the top of the stairs, turned left, and ran out of view.

I puffed my way to the top with Bruce on my heels. Of course, he was in top athletic shape.

We turned left at the top into a hallway with guest room doors on both sides. Paw crouched in front of one, scratching at the bottom of the door.

I opened my mouth to call Paw, but Bruce placed a hand on my arm and shook his head. The doorknob rattled, and the door swung inward. Madeline Wells stepped into the doorway, looking down at Paw.

"What are you doing there?" She crooned. Madeline stretched out her hand and Paw raised his head to sniff her fingers.

Bruce patted my back and tilted his head toward Madeline. His way of telling me to continue toward them.

I hurried down the hall, saying, "I'm so sorry. Is he bothering you?"

Madeline smiled up at me as she stroked Paw's back. "Not at all. He's a sweetheart."

Madeline appeared to have regained her composure from her early morning discovery. She wore a soft pink sweater with gray pants. Her hair was pulled back from her face in a chignon, and she wore a light dab of cosmetics.

"My name is Clarissa Hayes, and this is my boyfriend, Bruce Sever." I motioned to Paw with my hand. "And this is Paw. His full name is Paudius Pernivious."

"What a cute nickname. Paw. I like it." She crooned to him. "I like you, big sweetie."

Paw grinned and woofed his thanks.

All three of us laughed.

Madeline did a quick up down of Bruce. "Are you here for the murder mystery game?"

"I've been roped into playing a part by Clarissa." He winked.

I huffed, but fortunately neither Madeline nor Bruce heard me. Bruce was overprotective and a bit jealous. He didn't like me talking with other good-looking men. And yet, now he was pouring on the charm to Madeline, who was lapping it up.

"Oh, I love mystery party games. Karen, that's my friend, you'll meet her later on, always goes with me."

Bruce subtly shifted into private eye mode. "Is that why you chose to stay at Peaceful Dreams?"

"Definitely. I'm sure the town is nice, although I haven't explored it yet. The game is our main attraction." Madeline giggled. "I've solved most of the murder mysteries I've participated in."

I wondered if the game had something to do with her late-night visit to the kitchen. Perhaps she hadn't been going for milk but was searching for mystery clues when she found Cafferty's body.

Bruce nudged my foot with his own, signaling me to join the conversation. Since he was playing a version of good cop, I decided to be bad cop.

"Is that why you were in the hall in the middle of the night? You did find Cafferty, right?"

Madeline stopped laughing mid-giggle and glared at me. "I went for some milk though it's none of your business."

I lifted my chin. "You could have been searching for clues before the official game time started."

She unclenched her jaw and said, "I don't cheat."

Hmm. I wondered if that were true.

Bruce jumped into the conversation. "You found the body? You must have been terrified."

Madeline turned to Bruce with tears in her eyes. I doubted they were real. She touched Bruce's arm. "You have no idea. It was horrible. That poor man was crumpled at the foot of the stairs. All I could do was scream because I was frozen with terror."

Bruce patted her hand with sympathy.

I looked down to gauge Paw's reaction, but he wasn't

there. Where had he gone? I tried to glance behind Madeline into her room without catching her attention. Paw was in the room with his head stuck under one of the beds.

The guest room contained twin beds with a central nightstand between them. To the left, I could see the edge of a chair under a window.

I must have shifted enough to catch Madeline's attention. She glared at me then glanced behind her to see what I had been observing.

She saw Paw and rushed over to him. "No!" She grabbed for his collar, pulling him out from under the bed.

Paw struggled in her grip, stepping on Madeline's foot.

She yelped, released her grip, and sat down on the bed. "Get that mutt out of here!"

Paw ran to me and leaned against my leg. I patted his side, whispering, "Good dog."

Bruce stepped in front of me. "Can I help you?" He bent on one knee and reached for her foot.

She slapped his hand away. "No. Just get out."

Bruce gestured for me to leave the room.

I led Paw into the hall with Bruce close behind me. The door slammed behind us.

"That didn't go well," I said as I led Paw to the stairs.

"Maybe." Bruce scratched his neck as he looked back over his shoulder. "But we've learned that Madeline Wells is competitive."

"Enough to commit murder?" I began to descend the stairs.

Bruce didn't answer as he followed us down the steps.

We reached the foyer to the sound of more raised voices. *Now what?*

CHAPTER 8

Lillian Hardcastle stood in the foyer with Saber clutched in her arms. She was arguing with William. "I must see Clarissa Hayes now!"

Paw's hackles raised, and he rushed toward Saber who leaped from Lillian's arms and ran into the living room. Paw wrenched the leash from my hand and ran after him.

"Paw, stop! Come back here!" I ran after him as Lillian pushed past William.

"My poor darling," Lillian cried. "Get that big lummox away from my baby."

"I'm trying," I growled as I ran into the living room.

Saber had climbed to the top of a curio cabinet and perched there, looking down at Paw who stood up against the cabinet. The cabinet was made of oak and appeared well-constructed. Saber hissed and growled at Paw who barked up at the cat.

Behind me, I heard Patricia say, "My cabinet! Paw don't you dare scratch it. It's an antique."

Paw's feet were planted against the front of the curio, and I hoped he didn't damage the piece. I approached him from the side. "Easy, boy. Come here. Come on, Paw."

He turned his head to me with a confused look.

"It's okay, boy. You know Saber. Now come here."

Paw glanced back up at the cat, reluctant to let down his guard. By now I was close enough to touch Paw, so I stroked his back with one hand while I grabbed hold of his collar with my other hand. Bruce came up beside us and held Paw's feet as we eased them off the curio.

I examined the cabinet while Bruce held onto Paw. I breathed a sigh of relief. No scratches marred the surface.

Patricia and Lillian appeared at my side. Patricia peered at her cabinet, then said, "Thank goodness he didn't scratch the finish." She looked down at Paw. "Bad dog."

Paw backed up closer to Bruce.

Patricia relented. "Well, no harm done. I suppose Henry has gotten into trouble at times and will in the future."

Lillian huffed. "What about my baby? He's frightened."

Patricia glanced up at the cat who glared down at us. "Lillian, that cat can take care of himself."

She turned and walked out of the room.

Bruce handed Paw's leash to me. "Take him into the foyer. I'll help Lillian with Saber."

I led Paw from the room and met William just inside the foyer. He observed Bruce through the doorway as Bruce attempted to capture Saber.

William shook his head. "Better him than me. Saber can be a sweetheart when he wants to be, but when he doesn't..."

Bruce grunted, and Saber yowled. I glanced back and saw Bruce handing a wriggling Saber to Lillian. She cuddled him, and the cat settled contentedly in her arms. Bruce nursed scratches on his hand.

Shelbee strolled in the front door. Bruce stopped next to me, dabbing at his bleeding hand. I grasped his hand and examined the scratches.

Shelbee said, "Those need to be cleaned."

I nodded. "We'll go to the bathroom." I gestured to the door next to the living room. I turned to Shelbee. "Can you take Paw for a while? He had an altercation with Saber." I tilted my head to the living room.

"No problem." She took the leash from my hand. "Hey, big guy. Let's go see how Sammy is doing."

Paw looked up at me.

"It's okay." I stroked his ear. "I'm not mad, and I'm sure Samuel misses you."

He slurped my cheek then followed Shelbee as she led him out of the foyer.

Lillian came out of the living room. Saber purred in her arms. "Are you ready to find out about that bracelet?"

I stared at her in confusion. "What bracelet?"

"The one we found last night!" She grumbled to

herself. “Young people. Got their minds on useless things.”

I stiffened. “Lillian. What are you talking about?”

“The bracelet we found around Saber's neck. We've got to find who put it on him.”

Ah. Now I remembered.

Bruce raised an eyebrow, and William coughed to get attention.

“Care to explain that?” William asked.

Lillian glared at him. “It's none of your business.”

Instead of being insulted, William just shrugged. “Sounds like a mystery. I like mysteries.”

“Meow.”

“See.” William pointed to the cat. “He agrees with me.”

William stretched out a hand to Saber. I drew in a quick breath because I was afraid Saber would scratch him. Instead, the cat sniffed his fingers then turned his head and rubbed against William's hand.

If one thing could melt Lillian's cranky demeanor, it was Saber's approval of someone. Lillian stepped closer to William. “It happened last night...”

I ignored Lillian's recap of our nighttime search for Saber and guided Bruce to the bathroom.

The bathroom, a throwback to earlier years, was a tight fit. Bruce and I took up all the room. The toilet butted against my legs while Bruce's back was to the door with barely an inch between us. Normally I wouldn't complain about being so close to him, but it left little room to clean his hand.

"My hand's fine." Bruce eased his arm around me. "But a kiss would help."

I smiled as I stood on tiptoes and brushed a kiss on his mouth.

"I was hoping for a deeper kiss."

I gave him a playful shove. "I know you were, but anyone could come past." He hadn't pushed the door shut. "Besides, your hand needs some ointment."

"And you want to find out what Lillian is up to." Bruce knew me very well.

"She needs our help," I protested as I applied ointment to his hand.

"Lillian Hardcastle can take care of herself."

"Not with this." I recapped our search for Saber and the discovery of the diamond bracelet.

Bruce waited for me to put bandages on before he said, "Anyone could have lost a bracelet in the park."

I pointed to his bandaged hand. "And put it on Saber's neck? The cat couldn't have wrapped it around his neck and closed the clasp. Thank goodness it was loose enough not to choke him. Still, he could have gotten it caught on a branch and hung himself."

"That's animal cruelty."

"Yes. I want to find whoever did it and stop them."

When I finished putting away the bandages and the ointment Bruce backed out of the room. We returned to the foyer where Lillian and William were talking.

She turned to me. "William agrees with me."

William put up his hands in a placating gesture and

then stepped back. "I hear Patty calling me." He strode from the room with his head down.

"Hmph." Lillian pointed at Bruce. "Is he going to help us?"

I grabbed his arm before he bolted. "He is."

Bruce's muscles tensed. "What do you want us to do, Lillian?"

"Search the park of course."

"For what?" Bruce stepped back as Saber swiped at him.

"Don't upset my baby!"

I stepped between her and Bruce. "We'll help search, Lillian, but did you report this to Harry. This could be a case of animal cruelty, and Harry needs to know about that bracelet. It could be stolen."

"I tried but that Cheryl Hobbs was there."

Cheryl Hobbs was Harry's new dispatcher since Alma quit after she married Harry.

Lillian huffed. "She wouldn't let me speak to Harry. Claimed he was out investigating a crime and couldn't be reached."

Since Harry had been here on a murder case, Cheryl was telling the truth. That hadn't appeased Lillian.

"If Alma was still running things, she would have gotten hold of the chief right away."

I doubted that, but I didn't voice my opinions.

I cleared my throat. "Did you give her the bracelet?"

"No."

Bruce grunted. "Why not?"

"I don't trust Cheryl."

I extended my hand. "Can I see it?"

Lillian stared at my outstretched hand for so long that I figured she didn't have it with her. Then she stuck her hand in her pocket, pulled it out, and placed it on my palm.

The tennis bracelet had a single strand of sparkling stones. The diamonds, if indeed they were diamonds, twinkled and refracted the light from the chandelier. I examined the lobster claw clasp and ring. They were in excellent condition. No marks marred the bracelet, except for a tiny flower shape etched on the back side of the claw clasp.

"We need to give this to Harry."

Lillian snatched it from my hands. "You're not giving it to Cheryl."

"I wasn't going to."

Lillian put the bracelet in her pocket. "Since Harry is busy, I'll find who did this."

Lillian marched to the front door.

Bruce nodded in her direction. "Go with her. I'll call Harry and catch up to you. Perhaps he'll know of a missing bracelet or similar incident."

I gave him a quick kiss and hurried after Lillian who was striding down the front steps with Saber in her arms. For a little woman, she moved fast.

I caught up with her at the end of the drive. I thought of Paw, but he would only upset Saber with his presence. For now, it was best to let him stay with Samuel.

"Where in the park do you want to start?" I asked as I trudged next to her.

Lillian frowned in thought. "Hard to tell. Saber could have gotten the bracelet anywhere."

"Why don't we begin where we found him last night?"

We walked in silence out of the B&B and down along Park Lane. Three tourists bicycled past us. Saber tensed as they struggled uphill but resumed purring when Lillian stroked his back.

Lillian led the way through the park gates and headed toward the area where we had found Saber last night.

Once we reached our destination, I looked around with hands on my hips. "How do you track a cat?"

"You don't. Cats are stealthy."

"I should have brought Paw. He could have sniffed his trail."

I didn't realize I spoke aloud until Lillian grumbled, "Big galoot. He scares my baby."

I doubted anything scared Saber.

As we stood there, a young voice called, "Here, Kitty, Kitty."

Saber turned his head in the direction of the sound with his ears perked up. Saber jumped from Lillian's arms in a graceful leap.

"Saber!" Lillian cried, but the cat raced across a stretch of grass and disappeared into the bushes.

"Come back here. Saber! Here kitty!" Lillian barreled after the cat at a speed I didn't think she could manage.

I ran after her as she disappeared through the bushes.

I heard the young voice, a girl, say, "Hi, Kitty."

"Meow."

Leafy branches pulled at my sweater and stuck in my hair as I navigated through the shrubs. I stumbled out to see Lillian standing with arms crossed as a little girl sat on the ground, hugging Saber. Behind them, a young woman wearing polka-dotted scrubs ran to them.

"Kara!" the young woman called, "Leave that cat alone!"

I caught up with Lillian and the little girl at the same time the woman did.

Puffing for breath, the woman bent over and spoke to the girl. "Kara, don't run off from Mommy like that." She placed her hand on the girl's shoulder. Saber hissed, the woman jumped back, then bent down again to protect her child. "Let go of the cat this instant, Kara! It's not safe to pet strange animals."

She glared up at Lillian and me. "Do something!"

Lillian huffed out a breath and glared right back. "Saber won't hurt her." Softly, she mumbled, "He only ever likes me."

Which was true. Lillian was jealous of the cat's affection for Kara, but it wasn't helping the situation.

"Saber has all his shots," I said to the woman. "He appears to like your daughter's attention. Perhaps they could cuddle for a while."

Both Mom and Lillian glared at my suggestion.

Kara broke the tension by saying, "Saber lost his new collar."

"No, he hasn't. He doesn't wear one." Lillian's toe tapped with impatience.

New collar?

"Kara," I knelt next to the girl. Saber eyed me with disfavor but continued to purr to the girl. "What did his new collar look like?"

"It was beautiful. Pretty sparkly stones. I put it on him last evening." Her mouth rounded in an "O" of surprise.

"Last night?" Her mother put her hands on her hips. "When were you out last night?"

Kara stared down at Saber, reluctant to look at her mother. She shrugged but didn't answer.

"Kara!"

"It was when you and Dad went outside to talk to Mr. Griffin."

To me, she explained, "He's our neighbor."

Her mom demanded, "Where was Tommy?"

Kara singsonged, "He was on the phone with his girlfriend."

Kara's mom rolled her eyes. "Your brother is supposed to be watching you." In a stern voice, she asked, "Did you slip out without telling him?"

Kara shrugged.

"Kara Amelia Jones! You know you don't go out by yourself. You're only six years old."

To us, she said, "I'm so sorry. I'm not a bad mom, honest."

Lillian pursed her lips, no doubt ready to dispute that, but I waved her comment away. "It can happen. What I would like is for Kara to tell me what happened last night and where she got Saber's new collar?"

Kara looked up at her mom who nodded her consent. The girl bent her head but began to speak, "Tommy was ignoring me, so I went out in our backyard. I was sitting on the back-porch step when Saber poked his head through some bushes at the edge of our garden." She paused to stroke Saber's neck. "I love Saber. He's nice."

I glanced at Lillian whose expression softened at the girl's words.

Saber angled his head for Kara to scratch under his chin.

"He meowed, so I went over to him, but when I tried to touch him, he backed away." The girl's brow wrinkled. "He never does that. He backed up some more, meowing." She looked up at me. "He wanted me to follow him."

I nodded.

Kara looked down at Saber. "I followed him through the Perch's and Cullison's backyards and into the park. There's a gate at the back of the park where you can enter."

I knew the gate she meant. As far as I knew, it was never locked.

"Saber ran through and waited for me to follow. Then he led me to the gazebo."

Everybody who grew up in Tranquil Valley had visited the gazebo. According to Uncle Harry, the gazebo was there when he was a child. A beautiful wooden structure with open-air sides. Its white paint was peeling, and several of the floorboards creaked ominously when stepped on. The park board in charge of upkeep had a fundraiser planned to raise money for the gazebo's restoration.

Kara's mom shifted on her feet. "I told you not to go into the gazebo." Worry lines creased her brow.

"I didn't Mom. I swear. Saber led me to the flowerbeds around the gazebo where those pink flowers are blooming. Dirt was on the walk and a hole was in between two of the plants. He stood by the hole and meowed. The bracelet was in there. I picked it up and brushed it off. Saber butted his head against my hand."

She looked up at us. "He wanted me to put it on him."

So Saber dug up the bracelet. But who buried it?

Before Lillian or Kara's mom could dispute her explanation, I asked, "Kara, can you show me where Saber dug up the bracelet?"

"Of course." She jumped up, calling, "Come on Saber," as she headed down toward the gazebo.

"Kara," her mom said as she trailed after her daughter, "slow down. Wait for us."

Kara ignored her mom.

Saber trotted along beside the girl, tail erect and ears forward.

I turned to Lillian, expecting to find a frown on her face. Instead, she wore a wistful expression.

Kara's mom spoke to Lillian. "That cat shouldn't run loose."

Lillian pursed her lips. "Neither should Kara."

They glared at each other.

I increased my speed and left them to their argument. Kara and Saber waited by the side of the gazebo. Kara hopped from foot to foot while Saber sat tall with his tail curled around him. As I neared them, Kara pointed to a small mound of dirt between two Impatiens plants. The lovely annuals on either side of the mound had dirt speckled leaves and scattered blossoms. Stems were bent, broken, or flattened on the ground.

I stepped into the flowerbed and crouched by the hole, careful to avoid disturbing the area. The hole, about four inches round and three inches deep, comprised the middle of the mound. Saber had dug with gusto for soil lie on the sidewalk as well as the surrounding plants.

"Thank you, Kara," I said as I stood up. "I have two more questions."

She squinted up at me and nodded.

"Did you put the bracelet on Saber as soon as you found it?"

"He wanted me to. He kept butting his head against my hand."

I patted her shoulder. "I understand, but it can be dangerous for a cat to wear a collar when he's outside. Saber needs a collar that will break away. Do you understand?"

"If he gets his collar caught on a tree limb, it will break open and free him?"

I smiled. "That's exactly right."

She hung her head. "Saber can't keep the sparkly collar, can he?"

"No." I glanced at Lillian. "But he should wear a collar."

"A breakable one," Kara added.

"Yes. Perhaps you and Lillian can pick one out at the pet store."

Kara turned to Lillian. "Can we?"

Kara's mom spoke before Lillian could answer. "Kara! We don't beg other people for things."

Kara's smile drooped.

Lillian cleared her throat and sniffed. "Of course, we can get Saber a new, safe collar."

I dropped my head to cover a huge grin. Lillian had a soft heart after all.

"Yippee!" Kara cried. She scooped up Saber whose eyes bugged out, however, he purred as well.

Kara danced in place. "Can we go now?"

Lillian shook her head. "Clarissa has one more question for you."

Kara turned to me.

"Did you tell anyone that you found the bracelet?"

"No. Now can we go?"

"One more question."

Kara scowled. "That's three questions, not two."

Lillian laughed while Kara's mother blushed at her daughter's forthrightness.

"Sorry. I can't count I guess. Last question. I promise."

I raised my hand in a pledge. "Was anyone around when you found the bracelet?"

Kara scrunched up her nose. "No. I don't think so."

I crouched down to her. "Then do me a favor, okay? Don't tell anyone about the bracelet until Chief Harry investigates."

Kara's mom covered her mouth with her hand, no doubt catching the implication behind my request.

Kara frowned. "You mean Saber can't keep it?"

"No, dear," her mom placed an arm around her.

Lillian stepped up beside them. "Saber will be happier with a breakaway collar. We'll find a sparkly one. Let's go." She discreetly slipped the bracelet from her pocket to mine.

I accompanied them out of the park and over to Main Street to the pet store. I left them at the entrance to the store and walked in the direction of the police station. Bruce must have been delayed for he had failed to catch up with us in the park.

No sooner had I thought of Bruce than I saw him stepping out of the coffee shop. He held a brown paper bag and paper coffee cup tray in one hand and Paw's leash in the other.

Paw turned his head in my direction. "Woof!"

Tail waving, he dragged Bruce to me.

CHAPTER 9

"Paw! Slow down!" Bruce tried to juggle the drink tray without spilling but to no success. By the time he stopped coffee and tea dripped from his hand. The same one with the scratches.

As I hugged Paw, Bruce cursed as he transferred the tray to his other hand and shook his wet hand to dry his bandages.

Paw ignored Bruce's profanity and sat at my feet, leaning against my leg.

I took the paper bag from Bruce and pulled out a napkin then handed it to him while taking the drink tray. Half cups of coffee and tea remained.

Bruce scowled at Paw. "I love you, big guy, but sometimes..."

"You're not having a good day, are you, honey?"

He grunted.

"Let's find a bench, and I'll tell you about Saber."

We found an empty bench close to where we stood. Part of Main Street's beautification program included benches placed at intervals to create a hometown feel even though the town was already small. Mr. Cooper, who developed the idea, had lived in large cities all his life. He had a tough time accepting that he was in a small town now. Still it was pleasant to have the benches available.

Bruce took back the bag and opened it. He handed me a cruller while he pulled out a chocolate donut for himself.

Paw sat in front of us with big, pleading eyes.

"No chocolate for you, buddy," Bruce reminded him.

"Here, sweetheart." I broke off half my cruller and handed it to him. He wolfed it down in one bite. With a last pleading look at Bruce who didn't relent, Paw lay at our feet. Chocolate wasn't safe for dogs, but I suspected Bruce chose it so he wouldn't have to share.

"Saber?" Bruce prompted me before he took a huge bite of donut.

I raised one eyebrow as I bit into my cruller. Bruce could wait for a recap until I had a little sugar too.

Mm. I savored the bite then swallowed. "A six-year-old put the bracelet on Saber."

"You're kidding!"

"Nope. Her name is Kara, and Saber loves her. He dug up the bracelet from the flower bed by the gazebo." I recounted my encounter with Kara and her mom. "Lillian took the little girl to the pet shop to get Saber a new collar."

Bruce took a long swig of coffee while he thought. "So, who buried the bracelet?"

"I don't know, but I have the bracelet and plan to drop it off at the police station." I finished my cruller and licked my fingers.

"I haven't heard of any jewel thefts. You?"

"No, and as far as I know, no one has lost a bracelet. I can ask Alma though. The church ladies usually know all the gossip."

"Diamonds," Bruce mused as he swigged more coffee. "If they're real."

"Harry can have Seth Hammond examine them." Seth was our local jeweler.

Paw's ears perked up and he swiveled his head to our left.

"No comment!" Karen Taylor said over her shoulder as she shoved through the door of the shop nearest our bench.

Right behind her Mark Carter followed saying, "But you did know the deceased."

Paw jumped up at their loud voices.

"Woof! Woof!"

I shushed him.

Carter, our local reporter, was tenacious when he followed a story. With the police response to the death at the inn, it didn't surprise me that Mark was on the story.

"I'm not the only one!" Karen spotted me and marched over.

Paw moved in front of me.

Carter followed, asking, "What do you mean, not the only one?"

Karen stopped a few feet away when she saw Paw, and said, "Shelbee told me you investigate suspicious deaths. Maybe you better ask your dear William about his past with Cafferty."

She flipped her hair over her shoulder and strode off.

Mark jerked his head between Karen and me, trying to decide who to pursue. He gave me a nod and hurried after Karen.

"What did she mean? Did she know Cafferty? Did William?" Bruce stuck his empty cup into the paper bag.

"I don't know, but I want to find out before Mark does. Let's go back to the B&B and talk with William."

Bruce threw our trash in one of the new trash cans positioned at intervals along the sidewalk. He set a brisk pace out of town, along Curzon Street, and up the hill to the B&B. Paw trotted by his side without pausing to sniff out interesting scents. My pooch was on the case too.

I huffed and puffed the last way up the hill and into the driveway. Uncle Harry stood on the porch with his arm raised to knock.

"Hey, Harry!" Bruce called out to him.

Harry turned in our direction and waited until we joined him on the porch. "What are you doing here?"

"Hello, Uncle, good to see you too." I panted as I sat on

the top step. Paw flopped down next to me after he greeted Harry and sniffed my uncle's shoes.

"We need to talk," Bruce told Harry as he wiggled his fingers at me.

I gave him a "what-do-you-want" look.

"Bracelet."

I pulled the diamond bracelet from my pocket and handed it to him.

He handed it to Harry who asked, "What's this?"

Bruce explained about Saber and the buried bracelet.

Harry turned it over in his hands. "You think it's real diamonds?"

I stood up. "One way to find out. Ask Seth."

Harry nodded. "Good idea. I'll drop the bracelet off to him later. But now I have business here. You never did say what you two are doing here."

Bruce's attempt at distraction hadn't worked, so he opted for the direct approach. "Clarissa and I were eating donuts on a bench on Main Street when Karen Taylor stormed out of a shop with Mark Carter on her heels."

Harry cursed. "Mark is a pest."

Bruce shrugged. "True. Karen saw us, marched over, and suggested we talk with William. She claims he knew Cafferty in the past. We came here to find out."

Harry scowled. "I want Clarissa out of this investigation."

"I know," Bruce said. "But she always gets involved."

"Hello!" I waved my arms. "I'm standing right here."

Both men ignored me.

"Better we keep her involved where we can protect her," Bruce said to Harry.

"Enough!" I raised my voice.

Paw jumped up and growled.

I placed my hand on his neck and smoothed his fur. "It's okay, boy. I'm fine, just frustrated at the men in my life. You excluded of course."

Paw licked my hand.

Bruce and Harry said nothing.

"Uncle Harry, why are you back?"

"William's prints are on the wine bottle we found in the mulch."

"How'd you ID the prints so fast?" Bruce asked.

"William's prints were in the system. We lifted prints off the bottle and ran them to see if anyone popped up. William's matched."

"What?" William seemed so sweet to me.

Bruce crossed his arms. "What was he in the system for?"

"Embezzlement."

Behind us, Jac cried, "That can't be!" She stood in the doorway. I had been so involved in our conversation that I hadn't heard her open the door.

Jac stepped onto the porch with a laser focus on Harry. "William would never commit a crime."

At that moment I realized how close Jac had drawn to Patricia and William. Since her mother died when she was very young, Jac had always seemed so self-reliant. She adored her dad of course, but she handled things on her own. I only hoped that her newfound devotion to the Innsmans wouldn't end up hurting her.

Harry raised a hand, palm out. "His prints were in the system connected to his arrest."

"The system is wrong." Jac crossed her arms.

Paw pushed past me and leaned against Jac's leg. She ignored him which was out of character for her.

I stepped up and put an arm around her. "Let's go in and ask William to clear this up."

Harry opened his mouth, no doubt to protest our addition to his interrogation of William. I stared him down. Jac needed to hear what William said.

As we stepped into the house, William came down the stairs. He grimaced when he saw Harry. Jac rushed over to him. William put a gentle hand on her shoulder. "It's okay."

"Woo-woo!" Henry lumbered into the foyer.

"Woof!" Paw wagged his tail.

Bitsy darted around Henry. "Yip! Yip!"

Paw growled at her.

Shelbee, who followed behind with Samuel, lunged to pick up Bitsy. "We'll have to work with Paw some more," she said, referring to his dislike of Pomeranians in general.

Samuel sat down next to Paw. "Woof!"

Paw barked in return.

"They're catching up on the news," William quipped.

Patricia walked in the front door. "What's going on?"

William waved his hand to the living room. "Let's go in there. We can talk in private."

Harry gave a curt nod. "You understand that this is official police business."

"I do." William put an arm around Jac. "I want everyone here to know the truth."

Jac's eyes filled with tears.

William gave her a reassuring hug. "Cheer up, sugar. It's not what you think."

Patricia cut across the room and placed her arm around Jac too. Together the three of them led the way into the living room. I was sure Harry would object to all of us getting in the way of his interrogation, but he followed the Innsmans and Jac without a word.

Shelbee, Bruce, and I brought up the rear with the dogs trotting along beside us.

Once in the living room, we sat on the sofa and chairs around the room. Bruce chose to stand by the front windows while William sat on the sofa with Jac and Patricia on either side of him. Harry sat on the sofa directly across from them. The better to observe William as he answered questions. Shelbee and I took two straight back chairs, side by side, at the end of the sofa closest to Jac. Our dogs lay down at our feet, Henry across Patricia's foot, and Samuel and Paw at my feet with Bitsy on Shelbee's lap.

Harry flipped open his notebook. "William Innsman, can you explain to me why your fingerprints were on the wine bottle we found hidden in your mulch pile? The same bottle you denied knowledge of earlier this morning when I questioned you?"

Patricia harrumphed. "How do you know those prints are William's?"

"Because they are on record."

William cleared his throat. "Perhaps it would be best if I explained everything from the beginning then you can ask your questions."

Harry frowned but nodded his agreement.

"I knew who Cafferty was before he showed up at the B&B for the weekend." William sighed. "When I was a young man, just starting out in my first job, I met Thomas Cafferty. He was a fellow employee at the bank where I worked. At the time I was casual friends with him. We had a drink or two after work and would talk about the sports games and so on around the water cooler. I had no idea what a ruthless man he could be.

"Our boss, Mr. Sanderson, was a genial sort with one of the most beautiful daughters I had ever met. Her name was Penelope and I was smitten. To win her favor, and I admit, satisfy my ambition, I worked overtime to rise in the company. I figured if I impressed her father then I would have a chance at winning the girl. And I did. I impressed Penelope and her father. I was promoted to junior management and Penelope and I became engaged."

William paused a moment, lost in thought.

Harry shifted in his seat. It roused William from his inner world.

"What I didn't know was that Cafferty wanted Penelope and my job. He set me up. He embezzled funds from the bank, falsified evidence that I was the culprit, and tipped the police to the crime. I was arrested. That's why my prints are on file.

"Mr. Sanderson visited me in jail. He offered me a way out. He said that he would drop all the charges in exchange for me breaking off the engagement with Penelope. I told him to go jump in a lake. But when I was released on bail, Penelope would have nothing to do with me. Worse, Sanderson threatened to blackball me from employment in any bank. And he could do it.

"I'm not proud to admit this, but I accepted his deal. The charges were dropped, and I packed up and left the area. Made a new life for myself. Heard through an old friend that Penelope got engaged to Cafferty. That's the last I knew of the man until he made reservations at the B&B."

Patricia reached across and took William's hand. She turned to the rest of us. "I knew about everything he's just told you. Cafferty was a wicked man."

Jac put her hand on William's arm. "I'm sorry."

William smiled sadly.

Harry crossed his arms. "That doesn't explain why your prints were on the bottle."

Patricia nudged William with her shoulder. "Tell him."

William stared at her and then turned to Harry. "No. It doesn't. I didn't embezzle money, but I'm not without malice. You see, Chief, when I realized Cafferty was coming, I decided to get back at him."

Harry sat up straighter on the sofa.

"I knew Cafferty had a passion for wine from our younger days. I counted on that because I was going to pull a little prank on him. At dinner last night I displayed a bottle of expensive wine." He nodded to Jac, Shelbee, and myself. "The ladies can verify that."

"He did," I spoke for the three of us while Jac and Shelbee nodded.

"I told everyone at the table last night about its discovery in the basement when we bought this house. I was counting on Cafferty's greed leading him to steal it.

"Patty and I love to search out flea markets. Some years ago, I found an empty bottle of the same wine at a yard sale.

"I'm not a connoisseur of wine, but Devon from our local wine shop is. He identified the bottle in the basement as a fine wine. Since I owned an identical empty bottle, I decided to play a prank on Cafferty. With Devon's help, we filled the empty bottle with vinegar and sealed it to appear like an original, unopened bottle. That's the bottle I displayed at dinner and placed in the wine racks in the basement. The original is safely stored at Devon's shop."

Harry stopped scribbling. "How did the bottle get into the mulch?"

"I don't know. Whoever stole it probably figured no one would look for it there." William glanced down at Paw. "Well, almost no one."

Paw wagged his tail as Harry scribbled in his notebook. "Did you plan to kill Cafferty?"

"No."

"But you lured him to the cellar."

"Yes, but I didn't push him down the stairs. I wanted him to take a drink of what is considered one of the finest wines ever created and choke on the disgusting vinegar taste. Not to kill him. I wanted him to suffer, even a little bit like he made me suffer."

Patricia squeezed William's hand.

Harry rubbed his jaw with his left hand while he studied William. "Why didn't you tell me this earlier when I interviewed you?"

"Because I was afraid that you wouldn't believe me."

Harry grunted.

When he didn't ask anything, I spoke up. "How does Karen Taylor know that you knew Cafferty?"

Harry glared at me but let William answer.

"She could have been one of Penelope's friends. My arrest was in the papers at the time. Maybe she read about it."

"So you didn't know her?"

William shrugged. "No."

Harry stood up. "That's all for now. I'll contact you if I have more questions." He motioned for Bruce to follow him.

I asked William, "Did you tell anyone about the wine besides Devon and those of us at last night's dinner?"

William watched them leave then turned to me. "Only

Devon and Patty knew about the fake wine. Devon informed the park committee that I would donate the real wine for the fundraiser next month, but he assured them that the bottle was stored in his shop's wine cellar."

Bruce strode back into the room and sat down on the sofa Harry had vacated. He opened his mouth, but before he could speak, the front door slammed shut.

CHAPTER 10

Tap, tap, tap. The sound of high heels on the foyer floor.

Jessica appeared in the doorway, a look of disgust on her face. "This dumpy town is a disgrace. Nowhere else to stay. I'm going up to my room." She announced to us then turned and headed for the stairs.

The sound of muffled tapping drifted over from the carpeted stairway.

"Well." Shelbee laughed. "One of the guests has returned. In case you didn't notice." She winked at us.

All of us burst out laughing. It cut the tension that had been hanging in the room. Bitsy yipped and turned in circles on Shelbee's lap while Henry barked excitedly.

I wiped my eyes as Paw stood up and nudged my arm. "I'm okay, boy."

Samuel, who had remained lying on the floor, sighed at the oddities of humans.

We comforted the dogs and Bruce said, "What else can you tell us about Cafferty?"

"Not much," William said. "Like I said, I never saw him after my arrest."

"Do you know if he married Penelope?"

Patricia answered for William. "He didn't."

William wore a stunned expression.

Mouth open, I asked Patricia, "How do you know that? Did you know her?"

Patricia laid a hand on William's cheek. "I'm sorry, darling, but I read some of the old letters your sister sent to you. The ones you refused to open that sat in the attic of our old house. I found them when we moved here." She turned her head to address the rest of us. "William's sister, Beth, lived in the area where William was arrested. They fell out and haven't spoken since that time, but she sent William frequent letters at first."

"Hmph," William grumbled under his breath. "She ordered me to take Sanderson's deal, demanded I think of the rest of the family and their reputation. I swear she thought I did it."

"Oh, darling, that wasn't true. And if you had only read her letters, you would have known that. Beth wrote that Penelope and Cafferty got engaged but that the engagement only lasted a few months. Rumor had it that Penelope found out Cafferty was engaged to another woman whom he dumped to marry her. Penelope didn't trust him, so she called off the engagement. Shortly after that, Cafferty left town."

Jac crossed her arms. "Sounds like Cafferty was a criminal and a con artist."

"I agree." Patricia patted Jac's shoulder then stood up. "I have to get back to the kitchen. Dinner won't make itself and I think we'll have guests to feed." She sighed and glanced to the foyer. "I better check on Jessica too."

Bruce put up a hand. "Before you go, do either of you," he included William with a glance, "know if any of the guests argued with Cafferty? Or acted as though they knew him?"

"Not that I can think of," Patricia said. "I didn't realize Karen Taylor knew him."

William stood up. "Same here."

I whispered to Shelbee, "Does Jessica like dogs?"

"No. She doesn't. Why?"

I winked and handed her Paw's leash then stroked Paw's back. "Stay with Shelbee, okay?"

Sad, puppy-dog eyes stared back at me.

I stood up and followed Patricia as she left the room. "I'll go up and check on Jessica for you."

Patricia smiled, no doubt grateful to avoid a grumpy guest. "I'll make a cup of hot chocolate for you to take to her. One for you too. Wait here."

Bruce materialized by my elbow. "You're going to talk to Jessica, right?"

He knew me too well. "Yes."

"Good. I'm going to call a few friends of mine.

Perhaps they can dig up some information on our suspects."

He gave me a quick kiss and left.

Patricia returned with two steaming mugs of cocoa. "Hopefully this softens her mood."

I nodded, took the mugs, and climbed the stairs to the guest floor. Jessica's room was at the end of the hall to the right. It was the bridal suite, the largest guest room that the inn had, the one she shared with Cafferty before his death.

A small table sat to the side of the door where I set down my mug to knock on the door. I could hear Jessica grumbling as she approached the door. She flung it open with a frown on her face and a hand on her hip.

"Yeah, what is it?"

I smiled and extended the mug of cocoa. "I thought you could use a cup of chocolate. It's been a distressing day for you."

She watched me with narrowed eyes then took a sniff of the chocolate smell wafting in the air. Her shoulders relaxed as she reached for the cocoa and took a sip. "Mmm. Tastes heavenly."

I picked up my mug and took a sip. "Hot chocolate is one of my favorite ways to relax."

She waved me into her room and closed the door. "Sit down." She indicated an overstuffed chair with a wave of her manicured hand.

I sat in the chair, and she perched on the edge of the

double bed. We sipped our cocoa for several minutes in silence.

Jessica spoke first. "I hear you have solved murders."

I goggled at her. "How did you know that?"

She waved her hand as if to dismiss my question. "I overheard your friend at dinner last night."

"Yes. One or two."

"Then you can help me. You can find out who killed Thomas."

My mouth fell open.

Jessica continued, "Thomas was furious that the Daytons were here. He said they're criminals."

"Criminals? What kind of criminals?"

"I don't know." Jessica chewed her lower lip. "Thomas wouldn't tell me. But I know it had to be one of them who killed him. Maybe both."

"Why would they kill him?"

"I don't know." She rolled her eyes. "That's why I need your help. You can investigate and catch them."

She took a long swallow of her cocoa.

I sat staring into my cup. *What should I do? Go along with her request?* After all, I was investigating already. Perhaps I could question her in the guise of helping her.

"I need to know about Cafferty — I mean, Thomas's — activities last night." Jessica raised an eyebrow. I hurriedly added, "To understand where or how he interacted with the Daytons."

She nodded. "Good idea. Unfortunately, I don't know

where he went. After dinner, I came up here and took a long bath."

"Did you both return to the room after dinner?"

She hesitated. "No. Thomas walked me to our room and said he was going out to smoke one of his vile cigars. I hate those things. They stink. It was so thoughtful of him to smoke outside."

Thoughtful was not a word I would attribute to Cafferty, however, I refrained from saying it. "Did you leave the room at any time?"

"Why would you want to know that?"

"Perhaps I phrased that wrong. I wondered if it was possible that Thomas came back while you were out of the room. To track his movements last night."

"Oh. No. I stayed in our room all night. Until that woman screamed and woke me."

"Okay. Did Thomas come back after his cigar?"

"Yes. Then we went to bed."

"Do you know when he left your room?"

"No." A few tears traced down her cheeks. "I didn't know he'd left the room until I woke up and was alone. I was scared with that woman screaming."

I thought about Shelbee's version of events last night. Jessica hadn't appeared after Madeline screamed. "Did you leave your room to find out who was screaming?"

Jessica's eyes widened. "No. I was too scared."

"Weren't you worried where Thomas was?"

"I figured he had gone to shut the woman up."

"But wouldn't you have expected him to be in bed with you?"

She glared at me. "What's with the interrogation? I'm not a suspect. The Daytons are the ones who killed him."

"Do you have proof that they murdered him?"

"No. That's what your job is." She stood up and stalked to the bedroom door, pulling it open. "You'd best get at it."

She thrust her cup at me, so I took it, saying, "I'll let you know if I find out anything. Or have more questions."

I stepped out of the room as the door slammed shut behind me.

I carried the mugs down the stairs to the kitchens. Perhaps I should have told Jessica that I wouldn't investigate for her, but since I was already questioning people, it seemed like an effective way to keep her talking to me.

Paw met me in the kitchen and sniffed at the mugs of cooled chocolate. "None for you sweetie. Chocolate's bad for dogs."

I dumped the leftover chocolate down the sink and washed the mugs. *Where was everybody?* I heard no sounds from the commercial kitchen. Patricia had said she was going to prepare dinner. *And where was Rascal? And the dogs?*

Paw woofed. As though he could read my mind, he walked over and sat at the door connecting to the back porch, looking over his shoulder at me in expectation.

I hooked on his leash and opened the door.

Paw sniffed the air before walking through the door. I took a deep breath, enjoying the smell of fall leaves, and stepped outside. Chrysanthemums in shades of red, yellow, and orange bloomed in the garden. Crickets chirped and hopped amongst the plants.

Paw ignored the gardens, instead turning right and leading me around the side of the building to the parking lot. Six vehicles filled the space, including Robert Roberts's.

Paw passed the cars, tugging on his leash toward the cluster of trees at the back of the lot.

Shelbee and Robert stood around one of the stately oaks that had grown here for decades.

Squawk! "We have a problem." Squawk!

"Woof! Woof!" Paw lunged to the tree.

I held on to his leash and staggered after him, nearly tripping in my haste.

"Ack! You, big galoot. Get away! Get away!"

CHAPTER 11

Shelbee turned with a frown on her face. "I penned Paw in the kitchen because he scared Pedro, who flew up there." She pointed to the brightly-colored parrot perched on a branch, three-quarters of the way up the tree.

"Pedro." Robert held up a piece of an apple. "Come here. It's your favorite."

Paw sat at the bottom of the tree, tail swishing back and forth, as he stared up at the parrot. "Woof. Woof."

"Hush, Paw." Robert's voice held a note of frustration. He glanced at me. "Sorry."

"I'll take Paw back to the kitchen." I grasped Paw's collar and tugged but failed to budge him. "Come on, Paw." I tugged harder and pushed at his backside, trying to shift him.

"Silly dog. Silly dog." Pedro taunted as he hopped from branch to branch.

"Grrr." Paw shot up and planted his paws against the base of the tree.

"Pedro, shut up." Robert wagged a finger at the bird.

Shelbee waved a dog treat in front of Paw's nose. He sniffed it but continued to watch the parrot.

From my right side, I glimpsed a black streak whoosh up the tree.

Squawk! "Ack! A cat!" Pedro scurried to the end of a branch with Saber stalking him.

"Saber!" Lillian huffed into view. "Where are you, baby?"

Robert lost all patience. "Lillian, get that cat away from my bird!"

Paw continued to resist my efforts to pull him from the tree. His tail wagged furiously as he stared up at the bird and cat.

Shelbee gave up tempting him and pocketed the treat.

Lillian scowled at Robert. "Saber has a right to climb any tree he wants."

Robert turned to glare at Lillian. "Not now, he doesn't."

Meanwhile, Saber advanced along the limb of the tree and out to the branch where Pedro sat. The parrot kept squawking which only drew the cat's attention.

I thought Saber was too heavy to climb out much farther than the end of the thick part of the limb. I was wrong.

Step by cautious step Saber began to shimmy out onto the thin branch where Pedro sat.

Squawk! Pedro flew from the branch, headed straight for Robert, whose back was turned as he argued with Lillian.

Paw lunged after Pedro, but I grabbed his collar and hugged him to me. He stopped with a whine.

The bird landed on Robert's back, digging in his talons for purchase.

"Ow!" Robert jerked and raised his arm, trying to reach Pedro to unhook him.

Shelbee rushed to Robert's side to assist him.

Saber slowly inched back along the branch until he reached a section that supported his weight. He sat up, tail curled around his feet, while he licked a paw and cleaned his face as though nothing had happened.

Lillian skirted around Shelbee and Robert to join me at the base of the tree. She stared up at Saber. "Are you okay, baby?"

Paw glanced back and forth between the cat and the bird. His momentary distraction gave me the advantage. I tugged him from the tree.

Shelbee threw me the biscuit from her pocket which I used to draw his attention.

Paw followed me, sniffing the treat. I led him back to the kitchen where he crunched his treat in contentment. Leaving Paw there, I returned to help Robert and Shelbee.

By the time I returned to the scene, Shelbee had

unhooked Pedro's talons and the bird perched on Robert's shoulder.

I glanced up the oak tree at Saber who continued to wash his face, purring. Lillian stood with hands on hips coaxing him to come down.

Shelbee pulled the back of Robert's shirt out and peered at his back. "You need to treat these scratches. Come up to my room. Pedro will be safe there."

I winced. Paw was partially responsible for Robert's injuries.

We left Lillian talking to Saber at the oak tree. The cat would come down when he was ready. I certainly didn't want to be the one to climb up to him.

Shelbee led the way inside and up the stairs to the third floor. Pedro balanced on Robert's shoulder, grumbling to himself. When Shelbee opened her door, Pedro flapped his wings, flew over, and alit on the sill by the open window. Fortunately, the window screen blocked his escape.

"Pedro," Robert snapped his fingers, "be a good boy."

Pedro ruffled his feathers but ignored Robert.

"Robert," I said as I sat down on one of the twin beds. "What did you do last evening after I left?"

Robert unbuttoned his shirt, exposing his back. Shelbee picked up a tube of ointment from the dresser and uncapped it.

As she smoothed ointment on his back, Robert said, "I dressed the mannequin body for the mystery game, checked on Shelbee and Jac, then went to my room."

"It's next door to the Daytons," Shelbee said as she examined Robert's back. She patted him on the shoulder. "That should do. I'll check it later tonight and reapply the ointment."

Robert pulled up his shirt and buttoned it. "I wrote a chapter in my book but fell asleep before I finished."

Jealousy twisted in my gut. I was struggling to write a mystery novel. How could Robert write with such ease?

Robert, ever perceptive, said, "The book's about acting. Lessons for new actors. Don't get discouraged, Clarissa. You'll finish your book. Persevere."

"Sometimes it feels like pushing a rock up a hill."

"All true accomplishments come with work and doubts."

Pedro flew over and landed on Robert's knee. "Squawk! Tell Kathleen!"

I smiled at the bird. "What are you to tell Kathleen about?"

Robert smoothed the parrot's chest feathers. "He means I'm to tell you about Kathleen's escape last night."

"What escape?" Shelbee asked as she sat down next to me.

"Kathleen woke me up, batting at my face. That's her favorite way to get my attention. Once I roused, she ran to our door and scratched at it. I crawled out of bed, scolding her about ruining someone else's property. She howled so I opened the door because I feared she'd wake the guests or the dogs. Loud barking would be a rude awakening to paying guests."

Shelbee nodded.

"As soon as I opened the door, she scampered down the stairs. I grabbed a robe and ran after her. I paused on the second floor but didn't see her, so I continued downstairs. Muttering noises were coming from the living room. When I got there, I found her sitting by the French doors, meowing quietly to an opossum outside. The opossum trundled away when he saw me, and I scooped up Kathleen. As I turned toward the foyer, soft footsteps padded down the stairs. Curious, I peeked out. Madeline Wells tiptoed across the foyer and entered the dining room."

"Madeline!" She had lied to me.

"I sneaked after her. She crouched down in front of the sideboard, rifling through a drawer. Whatever she hunted she failed to find because she cursed and moved to the next drawer. I debated what to do. I hated to wake William.

"Kathleen mewled, and Madeline stilled, listening, then cursed again and hurried toward the door, so I ducked behind the reception desk in the corner. Cowardly, I know. She breezed past me and ran up the stairs. I heard a door close upstairs."

"Did you see anyone else?" Shelbee asked.

"No. I climbed the steps and paused on the second floor. No one was around, so I carried Kathleen up to our room and went back to bed. I planned to tell William in the morning, but then everything went crazy. There was no time to talk to him."

"Did you hear Madeline scream?"

"I think everyone in the county heard her scream. That woman would be perfect for the stage."

I scrunched my brow.

"She can project." Robert motioned to his throat. "Her voice could reach throughout the theater." As Robert was an accomplished actor, he should know.

Shelbee shifted next to me. "What took you so long coming downstairs?"

"Kathleen. As soon as I heard the screams, I jumped out of bed. Kathleen wound around my feet, tripping me in the dark. By the time I righted myself, she was at the door. Refusing to budge. Of course, each time I nudged her back, she slipped around me back to the door. I had to chase her and pen her in her carrier before I could leave the room."

I smiled at the thought of a big guy chasing after a little cat. She had him wrapped around her paw. "Did you pass anyone on the way downstairs?"

"No."

"Where was James?" I mused.

"You mean Dayton?" Robert shrugged.

"He's the only one in the inn that no one has mentioned seeing when you all found Madeline."

Shelbee tilted her head in thought. "He could have been sleeping off all the wine he drank at dinner. Maybe he never heard the screams."

Robert snorted. "Those screams could wake the dead."

Before Shelbee could argue his point, someone knocked on the door.

Pedro squawked and flew to the top of the armoire in the corner.

"Yes?" Shelbee stood up.

"It's me." Jac opened the door and peeked around it. "Clarissa?"

"I'm here."

"For goodness' sake, come in Jac." Shelbee waved her over to us.

"I can't. I've got Rascal with me."

The cat, who was cradled in Jac's arms, poked his head around the door.

"Cat! Cat! Help!" Pedro hopped from foot to foot.

Rascal's eyes widened, and he gathered himself to lunge from Jac's arms. She held tight to him, gritting out, "Stay here you, ornery cat."

She backed out of the room, saying, "Get downstairs, Clarissa. Bruce and James Dayton are fighting."

CHAPTER 12

I stayed motionless, stunned by her words. "What?"

"Hurry!" Jac called over her shoulder.

I ran to the door and out into the hallway with Shelbee on my heels.

Robert said, "Stay here, Pedro." The click of the door and heavy footsteps followed his words.

The three of us rushed down the stairs behind Jac, who lost control of Rascal.

He scampered past us up the stairs toward Pedro, intent on capturing the bird. I hoped Robert had latched the door.

As I stepped into the foyer, James Dayton swung at Bruce. Side-stepping the punch, Bruce grabbed James's arm and pulled it behind his back.

James cursed.

"Watch your mouth." Bruce pulled James's arm higher. "There are ladies present."

James glared over his shoulder at Bruce.

The front door opened and Uncle Harry sauntered in. "I see you have the situation under control."

Bruce grunted. "For now."

Harry strolled over and placed a hand on Bruce's tense shoulders. "Let him go."

Bruce raised an eyebrow. "Why? He needs to learn some manners."

"Let him go." Harry's soft voice held a note of steel.

Bruce glanced at me.

I nodded.

Bruce released James and stepped back.

James glared at Bruce as he straightened and flexed his shoulder and arm. He turned to Harry. Pointing at Bruce, he said, "Arrest him for assault."

Bruce tensed, but Harry raised his hand in a stopping gesture. To James, he said, "Seems to me you both were culpable."

James's gaze drilled into Harry. Before either spoke, Donna Dayton rushed in from the kitchen hallway and grabbed James's arm.

"Ow!" He cursed again. "Woman, that hurts!"

She ignored his protest. "I apologize for my husband's behavior," she said to Harry.

"And what prompted said behavior?"

Donna shrugged. "My husband drinks."

"I'm not drunk." James glared at his wife.

Bruce shifted, drawing their attention. "You may not be drunk, but you're rude. You owe me an apology. And Clarissa."

Everyone glanced at me and back to James who said, "She's sticking her nose into Cafferty's death. She deserves what I said about her."

Ah. Now I understood. Bruce was defending me.

"And if you didn't have anything to do with his death then it shouldn't concern you."

Harry stepped between Bruce and James before a new confrontation could erupt. Over his shoulder, Harry asked, "What did he say about Clarissa?"

Oh dear. Now Harry was in protective mode.

I cleared my throat. "It doesn't matter what he said."

Bruce and Harry ignored me. Harry pointed at James. "Apologize to her."

James stood silent. Donna shoved him. "Do it."

He huffed. "I apologize."

"Now," Harry said, "go off and cool down."

Donna curled her hand in James's sleeve and tugged him toward the stairs. "We'll go to our room."

They skirted around me and climbed the stairs. Once they were out of sight, Harry spoke.

"What was that all about?"

Bruce rubbed a hand over his face. "I asked him his whereabouts last night. He told me to mind my own business then said the same about Clarissa."

"What else?"

"He insulted her."

I walked over to him and placed my hand on his arm. "Bruce. They're only words."

Bruce looked down at me. "He threatened you. Told me you had better stop sticking your nose into things that don't concern you."

"He threatened her?" Harry snapped to attention.

"Not enough to charge him with a threat."

Harry grunted.

"Maybe Jessica was right." I thought aloud.

"Jessica?" Shelbee asked as she walked over to me. "What about her?"

"She told me that she believes Donna and James Dayton killed Cafferty."

"She got any proof?" Harry pulled out his notebook.

"No proof. At least none that she gave me. She claims Cafferty was furious to find the Daytons at the inn." I glanced at Bruce. "Jessica wants me to investigate."

"Well, you're not." Bruce crossed his arms over his chest. "It's too dangerous."

Shelbee tapped her chin. "But James is a hot-head. Seems to me he was running his mouth."

"So?"

"Bruce, if James truly meant Clarissa harm, wouldn't he have attacked her?"

Bruce's jaw clenched. "We're not waiting to find out. I'll investigate."

Harry cleared his throat. "That's my job."

I threw my hands up in the air. "Enough. We all investigate. Like Shelbee said, James is a hot-head. He mouths off a lot, but I'm not running and hiding from this case."

Harry opened his mouth, but I spoke before he could. "Uncle, I love you. And I know it's police business. But the guests will tell me things they won't tell you."

Harry closed his mouth with a scowl.

Robert coughed. "If I may, has anyone determined the time Cafferty died? I mean, did Madeline find him right away or was there a lapse of time?" He shook his head. "I'm not explaining this right. If James killed him, it seems to me it would have been in a fit of rage. I never heard raised voices or fighting before Madeline screamed. Did any of you?"

Silence filled the foyer. We had been so intent on Madeline's screaming that we hadn't considered the events of the death.

"I'll speak with Hal immediately." Harry turned on his heel. As he opened the front door, he said, "Thank you, Robert."

"You're welcome," Robert called as Harry shut the door behind himself. To us, he said, "Who's Hal?"

"The coroner." Jac bent to pick up Rascal who had joined us in the foyer.

"Where are the dogs?" Shelbee asked Jac.

"In the kitchen with Paw."

"Thank goodness," Robert spoke softly, no doubt thinking of Pedro.

I focused on Bruce. "We need to question the Daytons, but your altercation poses a problem."

He grunted.

"Let me talk with them," Robert said from behind me.

As I said, "Robert, we don't want to get you involved," Bruce said, "Good idea."

Shelbee nodded her agreement.

But Jac shook her head. "Wait until he calms down. We're preparing dinner now. You can talk to them after we eat."

"But," Shelbee asked, "at dinner, aren't we going to suggest to the guests that the mystery game continue?"

"What?" Robert crossed his arms over his chest. "That's in poor taste. A man is dead."

"Then you think of a way to keep them here." Shelbee sighed. "Harry wants us to keep them in town, and Madeline wants to continue the game. We thought the game was a clever way to find the killer."

"We?" Robert asked as Bruce said, "Or the killer to strike again."

Shelbee ignored Bruce while gesturing to Jac and me. "We."

Before either man could object further, the front door opened. Lillian walked in and stopped with hands on hips. "There you are."

The five of us glanced at each other wondering who she meant.

"I know who the bracelet belongs to."

"What bracelet?" Robert asked in confusion.

Lillian hmphed. "The bracelet Saber found. Try to keep up, actor man."

Footsteps tapped down the hall. Patricia entered the foyer and smiled at Lillian. "You'll stay for dinner," she told the older woman in a voice that brooked no argument.

Lillian huffed, but I caught a glimpse of a small smile. "Who's going to get Saber down?"

Patricia waved her hand. "Saber will get down himself; you know that. Now go into the living room with Clarissa and rest a bit. Dinner will be ready in a half-hour." She turned to Jac. "I could use your help, dear."

Jac smiled and nodded.

"I'll help too." Shelbee followed them as they went to the kitchen.

"Come on, Lillian, let's go in the living room." I led the way.

Behind me, Robert said, "I'll check on Pedro."

I turned to the living room. "By the way, how did it go with Kara? Did you choose a new collar for Saber?"

"Of course." Lillian followed me, her light footsteps barely making a sound. Heavier steps followed hers. Bruce had decided to join us.

I sat down on the sofa and moved over for Lillian to sit. "What did you buy?"

She sat on the edge of the seat. "That's not important now."

Bruce sat across from us.

"Who owns the bracelet?" I shifted to get comfortable.

"And how did you find out?" Bruce crossed his left ankle over his right leg.

Lillian crossed her arms and glared at Bruce. "Do you think an old woman can't play detective?"

I hid a smile as Bruce fidgeted under her stare. "No, ma'am."

Lillian uncrossed her arms and sat back. "You can learn a lot from church. The church ladies are an excellent source of information."

"Gossips," Bruce mumbled.

"Young man, that is unkind. Those ladies offer their time and service to the community."

I touched her arm. "But you've called them gossips in the past."

"I can. I'm older." She snickered. "They do love to talk." She sobered. "Which is helpful when you have questions and need answers."

Bruce raised an eyebrow but wisely kept quiet.

I sat forward. "What did they tell you?"

"Joan Dever lost her tennis bracelet three days ago. She's been looking everywhere for it."

Bruce cleared his throat. "How can you be sure it's the same bracelet?"

"The marks on the clasp." She turned to me. "Remember the marks you pointed out."

I nodded.

"Joan's been telling everyone who'll listen about them. Hoping someone will return it."

"Does she have any idea where she lost it?"

"In the park. While jogging."

My mouth fell open. "Joan Dever jogs?"

"Whose Joan Dever?" Bruce glanced between Lillian and me.

Lillian answered. "Cal Dever's wife. The owner of Swilly's."

I added, "The restaurant south of town. Expensive."

"That's for sure," Lillian said. "And Joan has never jogged a day in her life."

"How do you know?" Bruce asked.

"Because she always wears high heels."

Bruce stared at us. "Always?"

"Always," Lillian and I said in unison.

"She's lying then but why?"

"That's what we're going to find out." Lillian circled her hand to encompass Bruce and me along with herself.

"Not we," Bruce said. "Clarissa and me."

"Bruce Sever," Lillian replied, "are you implying I'm too old to help?"

She'd neatly outmaneuvered him. No way could Bruce admit to questioning her age.

He gritted his teeth. "Of course not."

"Then I'm helping."

"How do you propose we discover why Joan lied? Question her?"

"Of course not, Clarissa." Lillian tapped her head. "Think. Who is Joan's best friend?"

I shrugged. "I don't know."

"You need my help. You're not a good detective," Lillian said.

My mouth dropped open.

Bruce sat forward, scowling at her.

Lillian ignored us and continued to speak. "Dana Harford. That's her best friend. That's who we'll question."

"Why?" I asked before Bruce could berate Lillian for her harsh words.

"Because Joan tells Dana everything, and Dana is a pushover. She'll tell us why Joan lied." Lillian nodded her head. "Now I need to check on Saber before dinner."

She stood up and edged past me.

After she left, Bruce said, "You're not going to let her help, are you?"

"And how do you suggest I stop her?"

Apparently, he didn't have an answer for he kept quiet.

Robert joined us.

"How's Pedro?" I asked as he sat down next to me.

"He's fine. He's watching a pair of doves on the windowsill."

"Robert," I said, "I'm truly sorry that Paw upset Pedro."

Robert waved away my apology. "No harm done. Pedro loves to tempt Paw anyway. He does the same thing to Kathleen."

Robert's black-striped, female cat was a darling.

The three of us turned to face the door as footsteps

approached. Shelbee appeared in the doorway with a tablecloth draped over her arm. "Where's Lillian?"

"She went to check on Saber," I said.

Shelbee held up the tablecloth. "We're almost ready for dinner. Could one of you fetch Lillian? And one of you inform our guests?"

Robert stood up. "I'll let the guests know."

"Coward," Bruce teased him.

"Hey, Lillian isn't too happy with me. Besides, I doubt the Daytons are eager to see you or Clarissa."

"Fine." Bruce stood up. "I'll get Lillian."

"I could get her." I stood up.

"No," Shelbee said. "Help me set the table, will you?"

"Okay."

CHAPTER 13

Fifteen minutes later the table was set as Jac and Patricia brought in dishes of food for the meal. We were eating family-style.

"Passing dishes of food fosters a relaxed mood," Patricia told me.

"Or projectiles to use on your table mate," William said.

"Not funny, dear."

Bruce escorted Lillian into the room as Jac and Shelbee returned to the kitchen with William.

Patricia pointed to a chair, indicating where Lillian should sit.

Bruce pulled out the chair and seated Lillian, who asked, "Why serve dinner? I thought bed and breakfasts only served breakfast."

I whispered, "Under the circumstances Harry wants

the guests to stay in town. We thought serving dinner would entice them to stay the night."

"Humph."

William entered, carrying a huge tray topped with a domed lid. Delicious smells wafted from it. Bruce stretched across the table and assisted William to place the tray in the center.

"Something smells good." James Dayton stood in the dining room doorway and drew in a deep breath.

Behind him, Robert followed with Donna. Ever the gallant gentleman, Robert had offered Donna his arm.

Patricia pointed out places, and Robert ushered Donna to her seat. James sat down without a glance at his wife.

"Excuse me." Patricia stopped as she met Jac in the connecting doorway, returning with a dish in each hand. "I'll feed Henry and give him his insulin. Will you turn on the dishwasher?"

"Of course," Jac said.

A flurry of activity at the dining room entrance drew my attention. Madeline Wells and Karen Taylor stepped through the doorway in conversation.

"A murder mystery game must have more than one body," Madeline said.

"Not necessarily." Karen brushed a strand of hair from her face.

"No. No. The first starts the game but the second triggers a turn in the investigation." She glanced at the rest of us and stopped when her gaze landed on me. "Isn't that true?"

I shifted on my feet. "I've never played a murder mystery game."

"But you've solved murders."

Karen nudged Madeline. "Let it go, Maddie."

I cleared my throat trying to decide how to answer.

Bruce intervened, saying, "It's not the same thing." His tone was firm enough that even Madeline subsided in her argument.

Shelbee and Jac brought in the last food dishes as Jessica appeared in the doorway.

William gestured to those of us standing. "Why don't we all sit down?" He pointed out seats to each of us.

Patricia came in as the last person sat down and took her seat to William's left.

The meal progressed in a friendly and relaxed manner. No one spoke of Cafferty's death though I imagined it was on everyone's mind. Jessica pushed her food around on her plate. James Dayton had a hearty appetite and ate seconds.

When everyone had finished the main meal, Patricia brought in dessert. Apple pie with ice cream. "Made from apples from the town's local orchard."

"Delicious." James Dayton patted his stomach as he took the last bite of his pie.

Jessica frowned and pushed her half-eaten pie away from her.

William stood. "I suggest we move to the living room. We have some things to discuss."

His words caused a pall to descend over the room.

While the guests stood up and moved to the living room, I helped Jac and Shelbee clear the dishes. Lillian joined us, offering to load the dishwasher.

Patricia bustled around as she put away leftovers.

"Can we help?" Robert asked as he stuck his head through the kitchen door. Bruce stood behind him.

"No." Patricia placed a lid on a bowl of leftover salad. "Go into the living room and help William."

Both men wore expressions of relief.

"Lillian," Patricia said opening the refrigerator door, "you can wait here if you like. William will take you home after the meeting."

"I'm not leaving. Not until Saber comes down from that tree."

"Still, you can stay in the kitchen during the meeting if you want." Patricia closed the fridge door.

Lillian stood with hands on hips. "Are you trying to hide something from me? I'll join your meeting."

Patricia groaned under her breath.

"That's it," Jac said as she wiped her hands with a paper towel. "We're done."

"I should check on Paw." I turned toward the kitchen door to the hall.

"He's fine," Shelbee said. "Patricia fed him and the others while Henry got his insulin shot."

I hesitated, so Shelbee nudged me. "You don't want to miss the meeting."

The five of us walked through the dining room, across the foyer, and into the living room.

Bruce stood by the windows. Robert sat behind the guests while William had taken a chair to the side of the sofa. Patricia walked over and sat in a chair beside him.

Madeline and Karen sat on the sofa while Donna and James sat on chairs across from them. Jessica balanced on the edge of a chair opposite of where William sat.

Jac took a chair near Patricia while Shelbee sat by Robert. I walked over to Bruce and Lillian followed. He turned around two straight-backed chairs for us to sit on then placed a hand on each chair in a protective stance.

William cleared his throat to gain attention. "We've had a tragedy occur here."

James snorted, and Donna elbowed him.

William continued. "Patricia and I would first like to apologize for what has happened."

Karen, who had been looking at her hands, jerked her head around to William. "Did you kill him?"

Madeline gasped, and Jessica flinched.

"No." William ground out.

Donna shook her head. "Then there's no need for you to apologize."

William bowed his head to her. "Nevertheless, we are sorry you have had to go through this ordeal." He paused and then said, "The police would like us to remain in town for the rest of the weekend. It has been suggested that we continue with the mystery game. My question to all of you is, do you want to continue with the game?"

"Yes. Let's continue." Madeline nodded eagerly.

Jessica jumped up. "How dare you? A man is dead, and you want to play a game."

Madeline's eyes glinted. "It's why we came here. Just because Cafferty died doesn't mean we can't finish the game."

Karen placed a hand on Madeline's shoulder and leaned toward Jessica. "We're sorry for your loss. But if the police want us to stay, I say we do. I, for one, don't want to appear suspicious by leaving. I vote we play the game to pass the time."

"What!" Jessica lunged for Karen who fell back to avoid Jessica's reach and tumbled off the sofa.

Robert grabbed Jessica around the waist to hold her back. While I had been riveted to the confrontation, he had moved closer to the combatants.

"Get off me!" Jessica pushed at Robert's arm trying to dislodge his hold.

Karen used the coffee table to lever herself up. She advanced on Jessica, raising her hand.

Bruce stepped between the women and in a firm voice said, "Calm down."

Karen took a step forward, pointing at Jessica with her raised hand. Her voice shook with fury. "She was going to attack me. I won't tolerate that."

Madeline tugged on Karen's jacket. "Please let it go, Karen."

Karen stopped, lowered her hand, and then sat back down.

Bruce watched her a moment longer then turned to face Jessica.

“Fine,” she said. “I'll play nice for now, but you better find out who murdered Thomas.” The last was directed toward me.

“We will,” I said as Robert released Jessica. She sat in her chair again with a scowl on her face.

Donna mumbled, “If he was murdered.”

William clapped his hands. “I believe we should take a vote on the issue of the mystery game continuing. All those voting to continue the game, please raise your hand.”

Madeline's hand shot up followed by Karen's. Donna raised her hand next, and when James didn’t, she nudged him. With a sullen expression, he raised his hand.

Jessica hmphed, a look of disgust on her face.

William looked to Robert. “Are you willing to perform?”

Robert nodded in agreement.

Jessica tried one last time to stop the game. She spoke to William. “What about you and Mrs. Innsman? It's your B&B. Do you really want to play a game after someone was murdered? How will that look?”

William raised an eyebrow and turned to Patricia at his side. She answered. “Perhaps the killer will be revealed in the game.”

Madeline gasped.

Karen jerked her head around to stare at Patricia, ignoring her friend.

I couldn't see Donna or James's facial expressions, but both sat up straight.

"What!" Jessica stood up. "Do you know who did it? Tell me now!"

Patricia held up a hand in a staying gesture. "I don't know who killed him. It may have been an accident, but maybe a game about murder will rattle the killer if there is one."

Madeline spoke softly to herself. "Maybe he—or she—will use another game clue like the wooden wine bottle."

Bruce, who had returned to stand behind me, grunted.

Lillian whispered to me. "Do you know who did it?"

"No," I whispered back.

"Hmm. Should be an interesting game. Perhaps I'll join in. Just so long as you remember we have to question Dana."

My mind blanked. *Dana?*

Lillian tilted her head. "You haven't forgotten about the bracelet already, have you?"

Ah. The bracelet Saber found. Dana was Joan Dever's friend.

"No."

William placed a hand on Patricia's shoulder. "We'll start the game tomorrow morning. You have the clues that were delivered to your rooms last night."

Madeline spoke up. "What about Cafferty's clues?"

Jessica huffed. "They're mine now."

"That's not fair!" Madeline turned to William. "That gives her an unfair advantage."

Donna nodded. "It doesn't seem fair."

"Neither does Thomas's death," Jessica said. "Nor playing this silly game."

William intervened. "Jessica, please go up and bring down Mr. Cafferty's clues. We'll share them with the group."

"No." Jessica stood with hands on hips.

Robert cleared his throat. "I can divulge the clues as I have the master list." He pulled a piece of paper from his pocket.

James spoke for the first time. "Why'd you have that with you?"

"Because William told me he was broaching the subject of the game this evening. I like to be prepared."

Madeline bounced in her seat. "What are they?"

Robert cleared his throat. "Actually, there were only one set of clues given to Ms. St. Clair and Mr. Cafferty since we didn't know she was coming."

Lillian leaned over to me. "Who's Ms. St. Clair?"

"Jessica."

Toenails scrabbled on the foyer floor.

"Woof! Woof!" Paw ran into the room, straight to me, with Samuel right behind him, aiming for Shelbee.

"Woo-woo." Henry followed with his long ears dragging on the floor. He plodded over, sat down at Patricia's feet, and gazed up at her with big brown eyes.

Paw propped his chin on my leg. I caressed his ears, wondering how he had gotten out of the kitchen.

"Yip! Yip!" Bitsy scampered into the room, glancing back over her shoulder while waving her tail. She crashed into Jessica's leg.

Jessica cried out and jumped to the side, stepping on Bitsy.

The little dog yelped in pain, which drew Samuel's attention. He barreled to her side, forcing Madeline and Karen to raise their legs as he ran between the coffee table and sofa.

Jessica, who was unbalanced on her feet, fell on top of Madeline, who screamed.

"Woo! Woo!" Henry wagged his tail and ran around the other side of the sofa. Donna raised her legs to avoid being hit and clipped James on the shoulder. He cursed.

Lillian doubled over laughing.

Paw tilted his head as he observed the scene. As Shelbee and Jac waded in to calm Samuel and comfort Bitsy, Paw joined in to help. He pushed between Jac and Shelbee, causing them to stumble into Robert who was trying to help Jessica off Madeline.

They all landed on the edge of the sofa in a heap.

Bruce grunted as he strode over and grasped Paw's collar, pulling him from the melee. As William tugged on Henry's collar, Bruce motioned for me to hold Paw.

William handed Henry to Patricia as I urged Paw back to my chair. Lillian rubbed Paw's back to calm and quieten him.

Bruce got a good grip on Samuel and offered a hand to help Shelbee up. Once righted, she bent and picked up Bitsy, soothing her.

The yipping and wooing subsided. William helped Jac up, and she took Samuel from Bruce.

Finally, everyone was settled.

Patricia voiced the question on my mind. "What caused all the commotion? And how did the dogs get out?"

A voice from the doorway spoke. "I can answer those questions."

CHAPTER 14

I swiveled my head to where Mark Carter, our resident reporter stood, lounging in the doorway.

He shrugged. "I came in the back way, and the dogs pushed past me when I opened the door to the hall."

"You!" Karen Taylor stood up with a growl. "Why don't you leave me alone?"

Donna, James, and Madeline turned to stare at her.

Mark shrugged again. "A murder has occurred. I want to talk to everybody."

"Eavesdropping," Lillian said to me. "That's why he came in the back way."

I nodded in agreement.

"And I want to talk to you." Jessica pointed to Donna and James. "There are your murderers."

James jumped to his feet, fists balled at his sides. "Liar!"

Donna's voice held icy calm. "How dare you. Why would you accuse us?"

Mark pulled out his notebook as Jessica said, "Thomas didn't trust either one of you. He believed you were both criminals and said he had proof."

James took a threatening step toward Jessica but was blocked by Robert.

Donna stood and placed a hand on her husband's arm. "We knew Cafferty in the past. He was the criminal, not us."

Jessica glared at Donna. "He was not. You're just trying to throw suspicion off yourselves."

Patricia clapped her hands. "Let's all sit down and discuss this calmly."

Donna nodded and sat back down while James remained standing. She reached up, clasped his wrist, and pulled. James resisted, staring down at her, then grunted and sat down.

Robert stepped to the side while Jessica subsided into her chair. Mark moved closer, but before he could ask a question, Patricia spoke first.

"Jessica, do you know why Mr. Cafferty believed the Daytons were criminals?"

"No. He never said why. But I trusted him."

In a deep voice, James said, "That was a mistake."

Jessica glared at him. "What's that supposed to mean?"

"It means that Cafferty was a snake. Trusting him was my mistake."

He glanced at Donna, who nodded for him to continue explaining. James bent his head then said, "I used to own a construction company. Built it from nothing to a profitable business. We did excellent work and the business grew. But I was too greedy. Refused to turn down work. So, when a huge job was available I bid on it. And won."

He paused and scratched his head. "We didn't have the money to do the job. And the banks turned me down because the loans we had were late in payment. I approached Cafferty. He agreed to lend me the money, except afterwards he demanded I give him a cut of the profits. He was a bank loan officer. It was illegal for him to get a cut. I refused so he went to the company who hired me and told them I was giving him kickback payments. They canceled the job. Without that job, I couldn't pay back the loans, and we went bankrupt."

Mark scribbled in his notebook then asked, "Who was the company that hired you? And what was your construction company's name?"

"Dayton Construction. The Hillman Group hired me."

"What bank was Cafferty working for?"

James didn't answer so Donna said, "First and Fifth National."

Jessica crossed her legs and waved at Donna. "What about you? Were you part of the construction company?"

Donna shook her head. "No."

"Then why did Thomas claim you were a criminal?"

Donna shot back. "Because he was an evil man." "I worked as a teller at another bank in town." She glanced at Mark. "Traders and Merchants Credit Union."

Mark nodded as he wrote.

Donna shrugged. "Cafferty was cruel to the point that he decided to ruin my career after he ruined James's business. Cafferty was blackmailing my boss at the bank. Your dear Thomas," she sneered at Jessica, "forced my boss to plant evidence that I stole bank funds. I lost my job and no bank would hire me."

Jessica frowned. "I don't believe it."

Karen Taylor spoke. "Believe it. Donna's right. He was a no-good you-know-what. My sister-in-law was engaged to him, and he dumped her for a richer woman. Then she killed herself. That was Cafferty's fault. He was the criminal." Venom dripped from her words.

"No. It wasn't." Jessica glared at Karen.

Before she could continue, Mark spoke. "Sounds like you all knew Cafferty from the past. Did you know he was going to be here this weekend?"

Madeline shook her head. "I never met him before."

Karen's loud voice overwhelmed Madeline's. "What are you implying?"

The Daytons raised their voices to compete with Karen.

"You—" James cursed.

Donna's voice overrode her husband's curses. "How could we know he was going to be here?"

The remainder of the conversation dissolved as Karen, James, and Jessica argued amongst themselves. Mark focused his attention on them but how he understood what they were saying was beyond me. Words melded and tangled as their voices competed to be heard over each other.

The dogs, agitated by the loud voices, barked and yipped.

A piercing whistle rent the room.

Momentarily stunned, I stuck a finger in my ear to try to regain hearing as the whistle sounded right next to me. I turned my head as Lillian removed two fingers from her mouth.

Silence blanketed the room as the guests stared in shock at Lillian. The dogs tilted their heads and observed Lillian with respect.

"That's better," she said. "Now as much as I love a good argument, your arguing is annoying. And pointless. Don't you know not to talk in front of a reporter?"

Mark scowled at her.

Lillian turned to him. "Mark Carter, wipe that scowl from your face."

She pointed to Robert. "Walk Mark to the door and make sure he leaves."

"I have a right to be here, Ms. Lillian." Mark's voice held a note of censure.

"No, you don't. You are on private property. Now go." She pointed to the living room doorway.

Robert slapped Mark on the back. "Come on. You know you won't win an argument with her."

Mark tapped his pen against his leg in agitation but walked out with Robert.

Donna linked arms with James. "We'll go up to bed now."

"But—" James's fists remained clenched.

Donna leaned over and whispered in his ear.

James grunted with a curt nod, stood up, and stomped to the door with his wife.

"What about the game?" Madeline addressed her question to William.

"We'll begin in the morning. Everyone will receive an extra clue as well."

Robert groaned as he stepped back into the room. He would have to prepare those clues tonight.

Madeline grinned from ear to ear. "Excellent." She grabbed Karen's arm and stood up. "Come on. I want to prepare for tomorrow."

Karen allowed Madeline to lead her away.

"Hmph." Jessica glared around the room. "Guess I'll go up too."

Once the guests left, Lillian asked Robert, "Is he gone?"

"Yeah. I watched him get into his car and drive away."

Lillian nodded. "Good. Now Clarissa and I are going to rescue Saber from the tree." She motioned to Paw. "Leave him with Shelbee."

I bristled at her autocratic demeanor. I was about to

tell her she couldn't command me when Bruce said, "Good idea."

He whispered in my ear. "Take Lillian home. Then come back. Please." His eyes held a note of concern.

"Coward," I mouthed to him.

He grinned.

I ruffled Paw's ears and spoke to him. "Be a good boy for Shelbee. I'll be back soon."

He wagged his tail and stared at me with sad doggy eyes.

Bruce held his collar. "Come on, big guy. Let's find the kitchen. I could use another cup of coffee."

He led Paw out with Shelbee and Samuel by his side. "More coffee?" Shelbee said as they left the room. "You'll never sleep tonight."

Patricia rubbed Henry's ears. "You need to go to bed too." She looked up at William.

"I'll walk with Lillian and Clarissa. If they don't mind?"

"That's fine," Lillian said as she started for the door. "Just don't scare Saber."

William shook his head and smiled at me.

We left Robert mumbling about clue writing as he helped Jac with Bitsy.

Crossing the foyer ahead of us, Lillian opened the front door. "Hello there."

William hurried to her with a frown. *Now, who showed up?*

Lillian bent and picked up a black cat. Saber. "I knew

my sweetkins would get down on his own," she cooed to the cat, who wore a sparkling purple collar.

William exhaled. "Good thing we left Rascal asleep in our bedroom."

"Nonsense," Lillian said, "Saber loves other cats."

I kept my mouth shut.

I shivered when I stepped outside. The temperature had dropped, reminding me cold weather would be here soon.

William draped a sweater around my shoulders. He helped Lillian put one on as she protested, "Don't treat me like an old woman." However, she pulled the edges around and cuddled Saber in its folds.

"Thank you, William. It's colder than I thought it would be."

"Your welcome, Clarissa. Patricia keeps extras around the house. She's always getting too warm and taking one off then getting too cool and searching for a sweater." He smiled at the memory.

We walked in silence past the park. We passed a few people finishing their errands. "Hellos" and "isn't it chilly" were exchanged.

Saber purred in contentment in Lillian's arms.

When we arrived at Lillian's house, she asked, "What time does the game start tomorrow morning?"

My mouth gaped open. "You want to play?"

"Don't be ridiculous. I want to watch. Should be amusing."

"Lillian," William said as he followed her to the door, "it may not be safe."

"Not safe?"

"We're playing a murder mystery with a possible murderer. He, or she, may use the game to kill again."

"Well, of course, the murderer might react. Why do you think I want to be there? You lot need all the help you can get."

William turned imploring eyes on me.

"Lillian—" I began.

She cut me off with a slash of her hand through the air. "Enough. No more 'Lillian.' I know it's dangerous, but the killer has no reason to harm me."

"Not yet," William whispered.

Lillian, who has sharp hearing for her age, said, "What harm could a little old lady pose?"

"And if the killer thinks you saw something during the game? Something that could identify him?"

"Or her." Lillian reminded me. "I see your point, but it's not stopping me. I'm coming to the game."

"Fine." William huffed out a laugh. "How am I going to explain this to Patricia?"

Lillian patted William on the cheek. "Just tell her you listen to smart women like her."

"Mreow." Saber protested the sudden movement that rocked his comfortable bed in Lillian's arms.

William shook his head and stepped back out of claw reach. "The game will start at 8 am."

He turned and stomped down the front steps to wait for me on the sidewalk.

Saber struggled and leaped to the ground, meowing to go inside.

Lillian opened her front door, and the cat walked in with tail held high. She patted my cheek. "I'll be fine. And then we'll question Dana. I know Joan Dever is up to something no good."

She crossed through the door and shut it behind her.

I sighed. Now I had Lillian to worry about too.

I descended the steps, joined William, and together we turned back to the B&B. As we walked, I asked, "How could you be sure your fake bottle of wine would fool Cafferty?"

"Still thinking about that, are you? Do you think I'm the killer?"

"Don't be ridiculous. I believed what you told us. I'm just curious. How many people would recognize that wine?"

William smiled. "More than you would think. There are lots of wine aficionados in the world. They may not be able to afford the finest of wines, but they know of their existence. Although I must admit, if Devon hadn't verified the real bottle of wine, I would have assumed the empty bottle I found was a fake."

"You said you found it at a flea market. Where?"

"Yes. Over in Merlot. Ironic isn't it? To find an empty wine bottle in a town named for wine and then find the same wine in our basement."

I stopped and stared at him as we passed under a streetlight.

He raised his hand. “Scouts honor. Merlot has a huge flea market event every year. Vendors from across the country come to set up.”

“Cafferty recognized the wine. You said he was a connoisseur.”

“Yes. He was, but he wasn't the only one. Donna Dayton knew the wine. Do you remember her reaction?”

I nodded. “She knew the year too.”

William rubbed his chin. “Yes. She did. That indicates to me that she's well-versed in wines.”

“I wonder if James knew, as well,” I spoke my thoughts out loud.

William shrugged. “He drank plenty of the other wine we served. Doesn't mean he knew much about them, though he did want to see my makeshift wine cellar.”

We were near the B&B. Lights shone in the living room and two upstairs bedrooms.

“Woof! Woof!” Paw trotted down the front steps and ran to me. He stopped at a hand command I'd learned from Shelbee. We were trying to teach Paw to approach me at a slower pace, so he didn't knock me down in his enthusiasm.

Paw slowed some but bumped against me. His tail whacked my legs.

Bruce strode down the steps with a mug in his hand. He inclined his head to Paw. “Big guy needed a walk before bed.”

I scratched Paw under his collar. “He can go on our walk home.”

“No. He can't.” Bruce handed me the mug.

I took a sip. Mm. Hot chocolate.

Paw shook himself, sending drool everywhere.

Bruce put up an arm to shield his face while William stepped away from me. “I’ll check on Patricia.” He waved and left Bruce and me alone.

“I’ll finish this.” I held up my mug. “Then I'll take Paw home.”

“No,” Bruce said. “We're staying here tonight.”

CHAPTER 15

I raised an eyebrow as my mouth was full of hot chocolate.

"I arranged everything with Patricia. You'll share with Jac and Shelbee, and I'll share Robert's room."

I swallowed. "Why?"

"Because I want to be on the scene if the killer decides to strike again."

"You believe Cafferty was murdered?"

Bruce rubbed the back of his neck. "Yeah. I do."

I smiled behind my cup of chocolate. "And you want me to stay."

"Yeah, well, I figure you'd just come back if you knew that I was staying."

I nudged him with my shoulder. "Irresistible, aren't you?"

"And you can't resist a mystery."

"Woof!" Paw's tail slapped Bruce's leg.

"You too, big guy."

I laughed at Paw's eager expression. "We're busted, buddy."

Paw sat down and tilted his head to me.

"Let's go inside." I shivered as I drew my sweater closer around me. "I need more hot chocolate."

"You go. I'll take Paw for a quick walk." Bruce tugged on Paw's leash.

Paw glanced between us then stood up with a sigh. He followed Bruce through the parking lot but glanced back at me every few steps.

I waved to him and hurried to the front door, shivering. I was enveloped in warmth as I entered the foyer, shut the door behind me, and listened. Distant voices conversed from the kitchen area. Otherwise, all was quiet.

I carried my empty mug back to the private kitchen where the voices were more distinct. I stepped through the door when I recognized Shelbee's voice say, "Whew! Dishes are done. I'm ready for bed."

Jac threw the dish towel into the laundry hamper. "Me too."

"Not so fast," Robert said, as he hunched over the kitchen table. "I need more clues for tomorrow morning."

Samuel lay on a rug in the corner with Bitsy curled up beside him.

Jac saw me enter. "More hot chocolate?"

"Please."

She picked up a carafe sitting on the counter by a toaster. I met her halfway across the room.

As Jac filled my mug, Shelbee said, "I've put an air mattress on the floor in our room and one in Robert's. Hope that's comfortable."

Robert glanced up from his notes. "Air mattresses?"

Shelbee nodded. "Clarissa and Bruce are staying here tonight."

Jac finished filling my mug and returned the carafe to the counter. She opened an overhead cabinet door and lifted down a tray. "I'll fix a few snacks to take up to our room along with the hot chocolate."

Robert scratched his chin with the end of his pen. "Why are Clarissa and Bruce staying the night here?"

I sat down across from him. "Because Bruce believes Cafferty was murdered."

"He thinks the murderer will kill again?"

Samuel raised his head, whined softly, then lay back down.

I took a moment to enjoy the sight of the two dogs before answering Robert's question. "That's his fear. He would never forgive himself if something happened and he wasn't here to prevent it."

The back door rattled. I jumped at the sound as Bruce and Paw entered. Paw trotted to me and propped his chin on my leg. I stroked his back which felt cool to the touch. "Bet you're glad to have a warm coat on, huh, sweetie?"

He rolled his eyes and sighed.

I unsnapped his leash and set it on the table.

Bruce sat down next to me and took a big gulp from my mug.

Robert tapped his pen on the table and asked Bruce, "What are your plans for stopping the killer?"

"I'm staying awake and patrolling tonight. That's the best I can do until I find out who the killer is."

Shelbee and Jac sat at the table.

Jac placed a plate of peanut butter crackers in the center of the table and pulled up a chair. "You can't stay up all night."

"I can," Bruce said as he took a cracker. "I've done surveillance lots of times."

"But you have us." Shelbee sat down next to Jac. "We'll take turns patrolling."

Bruce shook his head "no" before she finished speaking. "Too dangerous."

I sighed at Bruce's overprotectiveness.

Robert pushed his notes to the side. "I could watch."

"No." Bruce pulled the plate of crackers closer to himself. "You have to prepare for the game tomorrow." He glanced around the table. "You all do. I can sleep tomorrow while the game is in progress."

I stroked Paw's ears. "Don't you think the killer will attack during the game?"

"No."

Robert pulled his notes in front of him. "I'll finish these then since I can't change your mind."

Shelbee picked up one of Robert's notes. "I'll help Robert finish these then go up to bed."

Jac stood up and retrieved the tray on the counter. "I'm going to bed. Come on, Samuel. Come on, Bitsy."

Both dogs scrambled up and followed her out of the kitchen.

"I'll be up soon," I called after her.

I turned to Shelbee. "Do you think Paw and Bitsy will get along tonight?"

Paw hated Pomeranians. He was slowly accepting Bitsy, and they had stayed together in the kitchen with surprisingly no problems, but I wasn't confident they could share a tiny bedroom overnight.

Shelbee scrunched her forehead. "Maybe."

Bruce swallowed more of my hot chocolate. "I'll keep him with me."

"Where are you going to be?" I asked as I snapped on Paw's leash.

"In the living room for now. I'll patrol every so often. Paw will let me know if something is wrong."

~

I curled on my side watching Samuel in his sleep. Shelbee and Jac slept above me on the twin beds. The air mattress was surprisingly comfortable, but my mind wouldn't quiet.

Samuel's paws twitched as he slept. I wondered what he was dreaming. Perhaps he was chasing a squirrel in his sleep.

Bitsy was nestled in bed with Shelbee. The little dog huffed out a gentle snore.

I rolled onto my back. *What was Bruce doing? How was Paw?*

Click. The sound of a door being closed with care. To me, it reverberated in the silent night, and yet neither Shelbee nor Jac woke up.

Samuel raised his head, and Bitsy jumped down next to me. I sat up. Both dogs stood with ears perked, listening.

I picked up Bitsy and cuddled her. Time to investigate.

I slid off the mattress and stood up, jamming my feet into my slippers, and tiptoed to the door.

I turned the doorknob and eased the door open a crack, trying to be as quiet as possible.

Bitsy and I peeked through the opening. Samuel pushed his head in next to me. No one was in sight, but quiet footsteps faded away down the stairs.

Bitsy opened her mouth to bark, but I gently clasped her muzzle closed. Samuel whined.

I glanced between them. If I left them behind, they'd bark and alert everyone. Pulling the door wider I stepped into the hall, Samuel pushing past me. I closed the door behind us with a gentle snick.

The three of us padded to the stairs and descended. The halls were lit with strategically placed night lights.

When we reached the second-floor hall, I paused to listen.

Bitsy wiggled in my arms, so I set her on the floor. She yipped, and I shushed her. The little dog stopped mid-bark, giving me a reproachful frown.

Samuel, nose to the floor, tracked a scent. He trailed it to the stairs leading to the foyer and began to descend. Bitsy scampered after him.

I glanced around the second floor but saw nothing out of place, so I followed Samuel.

I stopped on the second step from the bottom and peered into the living room. No light shone from the room, but the moonlight through the window cast a swath of light across both sofas. They were empty. Silence filled the foyer.

Where were Bruce and Paw?

Samuel jerked his head up and turned to face the hall leading to the kitchens. Bitsy yipped and charged ahead. Samuel ran after her.

So much for sneaking up on whoever was creeping around tonight.

The dogs barreled through the private kitchen door.

As I ran after them, a female voice shrieked one piercing scream then silence fell.

I pushed through the kitchen door and skidded to a halt.

Patricia stood with a skillet raised in one hand as she fended off Samuel's kisses.

Bitsy danced around Patricia's feet.

I rushed over and pulled Samuel back.

Patricia lowered the skillet and set it on the counter. She held a hand to her chest. "You scared me!"

"Sorry. Samuel, sit!" He sat down and thumped his tail. "I thought the killer was creeping around down here."

Bitsy stood against Patricia's legs. The innkeeper picked up the little dog and cuddled her. "I thought everyone was asleep but me, so I thought I'd make some tea." She motioned to the canister of tea bags on the counter.

"I'll make us a cup. I couldn't sleep either. My mind kept running in circles over Cafferty's death."

Patricia sat at the table with Bitsy on her lap.

Samuel walked over and lay by Patricia with his head resting on her feet.

Patricia sighed. "I wish Cafferty had never come here. All it has caused is trouble."

I filled the tea kettle with water, set it on the stove, and turned it on. Taking a tray from the cupboard, I placed two cups and the sugar bowl on it. "Do you know where Bruce is?"

"No. I checked the living room when I came down. Thought Bruce would like some tea too. But he wasn't there."

I selected two tea bags from the canister and set them on the tray along with two spoons. "Most likely he's patrolling outside. He'll have Paw with him." I glanced at the kitchen clock. 2:47 am.

Patricia smoothed Bitsy's fur. The little dog smiled,

with tongue peeking out, at the attention. "Henry is snoring on his bed upstairs. He's as bad as William." She kissed Bitsy. "I'm glad they are safe."

The kettle whistled behind me, causing me to jump. I turned off the stove, filled two cups with water, and carried the tray over, placing it in front of Patricia.

"How much do you know about Cafferty?" I asked as I steeped my tea bag.

Patricia placed Bitsy on the floor, so she could prepare her tea. The little Pom yipped softly then curled up against Samuel's side. "Not much. I only met him when he showed up at the inn. I'd read William's sister's letters though. Cafferty was a horrible human being. I can understand why someone would kill him." She glanced up at me. "Not William though. I hope you believe that."

"I do, but it would help to know more about his life and past and the motives of the guests. Of course, his death could be an accident."

Patricia stirred her tea. "I wish I could help you, but I've already told you all I know."

A loud voice from outside said, "I have every right to be outside if I wish."

Samuel and Bitsy jumped to their feet and ran to the door, barking in excitement, as I stood up.

The doorknob rattled, and the door swung inward.

Karen Taylor marched in with Bruce and Paw following.

"Woof!" Paw joined in the barking.

Bruce scowled at Karen. “There is a possible murderer on the loose. Why would you want to be out by yourself?”

Karen shouted to be heard over the dogs’ barking. “Young man, I can take care of myself.” To the dogs, she commanded, “Shut up!”

All three dogs stopped barking and tilted their heads to observe her.

I smiled at their cute expressions, but Karen scowled.

Chilly air swirled through the kitchen. I shivered as Patricia called, “Shut the door, please.”

Bruce obeyed, locking the door then shrugging out of his coat. “What were you doing out there?”

Karen ignored him. “I'm going to bed.” She marched out of the room, her footsteps fading as she moved deeper into the inn.

Bruce glanced between Patricia and me. “Is everybody up?”

I hugged Paw. “No. Just us, unless the dogs’ barking woke someone up. We couldn't sleep.”

“Couldn’t sleep. So, you wandered around the house with a killer in it?”

Bruce's cold mood irritated me. “You are on patrol. Shouldn't we be safe?” I turned my back on him and sat down at the table picking up my tea.

Paw flopped at my feet while Samuel and Bitsy milled around the room, sniffing the floor.

Patricia stood up and retrieved another cup from the cupboard. “Come have some tea, Bruce. We ladies worry when our loved ones are in danger.”

Bruce sat down and accepted the cup of tea Patricia handed him. "Sorry." He mumbled as he added two teaspoons of sugar.

I nodded. "Did you hear Karen outside?"

"No. I patrolled every hour. Paw heard her when we were in the back garden. He led me to the corner of the house, and we met her as she came around the side."

"Good boy." I stroked his back.

Paw raised his head and whined.

A scream rent the air.

CHAPTER 16

"Not again." Patricia dropped her teacup. Fortunately, it landed on the table without breaking but did spill tea across the top.

The dogs barked and ran out of the room toward the sound.

Bruce ran after them with Patricia and me right behind.

Bruce climbed the front stairs two at a time and disappeared as he turned left at the top.

William, followed by Shelbee and Jac, descended from the third floor and met Patricia and I as we ascended from the first.

To our left Donna, James, and Jessica stood huddled together by an open door. Inside a woman wept.

I ran forward and pushed through their huddle. Karen

Taylor knelt by one of the beds on which Madeline Wells lay still.

Bruce felt for a pulse at Madeline's neck then looked up at me and shook his head.

She was dead. But how? And why? And who?

The dogs, noses to the floor, sniffed around the room. Bruce nodded to them. "Get them out of here."

I grabbed Paw's collar and tugged. He resisted, pulling against my hold, determined to sniff a pillow that had fallen to the floor.

He looked up at me as he pawed the pillow. "Woof!"

Bruce bent and looked at the pillow then back to the bed. He touched Paw's back. "Good boy. Now go with Clarissa."

I tugged gently, and he willingly followed. Shelbee and Jac had pushed into the room and helped gather the dogs while Patricia knelt and placed an arm around Karen.

William, arms spread, ushered the guests huddled in the hall away from the door. "Please go back to your rooms."

Bruce called to him. "I want everyone in the living room."

James balled his hands into fists. "Who put you in charge?"

"I did," Bruce lied as he folded his arms.

Jessica pulled her robe tighter around her. "I'm going back to bed."

"No," Bruce said, "you're not. The police will be here soon."

Jessica grumbled but stayed where she stood.

Donna turned toward the stairs, speaking over her shoulder. "Come on, James. We might as well get comfortable in the living room."

James glared at Bruce then turned and followed his wife.

"Humph." Jessica turned on her heel and walked away.

William said to Bruce, "I'll call the police."

I led Paw from the room and followed the guests who descended the stairs. With Shelbee by my side, cuddling Bitsy to her chest and Jac behind us, leading Samuel, we closed the dogs in the private kitchen.

Shelbee crooned to Bitsy. "Stay here, sweetheart."

"Good job, boy." Paw's tongue lolled out.

Jac set a bowl of water next to Samuel, who gulped it up. "I'm going up and getting Henry and Rascal."

"I'll brew tea and coffee." Shelbee set Bitsy on a cushion on the floor. "Are you going up to help Bruce?"

"Yes," I said, "and I'll see if Patricia needs help with Karen."

I turned to the door but stopped abruptly. "Wait a minute. Where's Robert?"

"Oh, no!" Shelbee cried. "What if the killer attacked him?"

Jac hugged herself. "I'll check if he's in his room."

"No," I said. "Let Bruce do it."

Jac and I slipped through the kitchen door, crossed

the foyer, and climbed the stairs. Through the living room door, I glimpsed the guests huddled in silence. William sat in a chair near the door.

I heard a faint siren. Uncle Harry would soon be here.

I turned left at the top of the stairs while Jac climbed to the third floor.

Patricia supported a sobbing Karen as they walked down the hall. "We're going down to the kitchen for some tea."

"Shelbee's preparing it. Why don't you go to the living room?" I nodded to a weeping Karen. "Can I help?"

Patricia shook her head. "We're fine."

Karen ignored me, too caught up in her grief. She clutched a wad of soggy tissues to her streaming eyes.

I met Bruce in the doorway of the room Madeline and Karen shared.

I shuddered as I looked at Madeline lying lifeless on the bed. "I wish we could cover her."

"Not until Harry gets here."

Louder sirens punctuated his words.

I worried my lower lip. "We need to check on Robert. We haven't seen him."

"Robert's fine. He left the B&B shortly after midnight. Pedro was squawking and fussing, and Robert felt the parrot would calm down if he took him home. He'll be back here early this morning."

I breathed a sigh of relief and gazed around the room, attempting to avoid the sight of Madeline on the bed. I tilted my head in thought. "Why kill Madeline?"

"What do you mean?"

"As far as we know she had no connection to Cafferty. And Jessica was the one accusing others of murder."

Bruce rubbed his chin. "Madeline wanted to continue the mystery game."

"Yes. But what harm would that cause? We were hoping the killer would reveal something in the game, but it was a long shot."

"We need to dig deeper. Perhaps Madeline was connected to Cafferty."

"And if she wasn't?"

"Watch the door," Bruce said as he pulled on latex gloves. "I'm going to search the room for any clue to Madeline's connection with Cafferty."

I glanced down the hall. No one was in sight, but the police sirens were louder. "You'll finish more quickly with my help."

Bruce grunted and handed me a pair of gloves.

I glanced around as I put a glove on my right hand. Twin beds with a nightstand between them filled most of the room. Madeline lay on the bed closest to the door. The other bed was neatly made with a floral-printed spread. The pillow we believed killed Madeline laid on the floor between the beds.

A plate of cookies and an empty glass with what appeared to be milk residue sat on the nightstand next to a lamp. The lamp cast the room in patches of light and shadow.

Bruce turned on the lamp on the dresser by the door, where a purse and assorted cosmetics were scattered.

Directly across from the beds was a closet, its doors partway open. A straight back chair by the closet held a large tote bag.

I pushed the handles of the tote open, leaving Bruce to check the nightstand and beds. I shuddered at the thought of searching near Madeline's body.

As I searched, I listened for sounds in the hall. I was anxious. When Bruce spoke, I jumped.

"Leave things exactly as you found them."

I rolled my eyes although Bruce couldn't see as I was facing away from him. I'd searched rooms before and knew what I was doing.

I picked my way through the contents of the bag. A mishmash of possessions included a hairbrush, lotion, shampoo, and underwear. As I delved amongst the bottom layer of clothing, my hand hit something solid. I pushed aside the clothes and grabbed the object, pulling it out. "How did this get here?"

"What?" Bruce stepped closer and looked over my shoulder at the gun in my hands. "That's not real."

The gun, made of wood, was carved in intricate detail to appear real.

"No. It isn't. It is one of the props that Hans Greble made for the murder mystery game. Shelbee showed it to me last night before she and Jac hid them for the game."

"Then how did it get in here?"

"I don't know."

"Mreow!"

Bruce wheeled around toward the sound, brushing against my shoulder. I peered around him at the doorway. Rascal strolled in with head held high and tail erect. He stopped and sniffed the air with mouth open. "Chuff."

"Did he sneeze?" Bruce asked as the cat twined around his legs.

"Yes."

"What's he doing here?" Bruce bent to pick up the cat who evaded his grasp.

"He must have run away from Jac." I wiggled my fingers to get Rascal's attention.

He ignored me and slipped into the closet.

Bruce cursed. "Get him out of there. He'll contaminate the crime scene."

I thrust the gun into Bruce's hands. "Here. Put this back under the clothes."

I pushed open the closet door and knelt on the floor, pushing aside two suitcases and three shopping bags stuffed with items.

No Rascal.

"Mreow?"

I looked up to where Rascal perched on the empty shelf above the clothes rail. He sat hunched over with his tail curled around his body staring down at me. A quizzical expression filled his eyes.

"Rascal. Get down here."

The cat purred but didn't move.

I jumped up and lifted my arms to grab him.

He edged back out of my reach.

"Here," Bruce said as he stepped in front of me. "I'll get him."

Rascal watched Bruce's hands rise and then sidled to the side.

Bruce followed.

The cat sidled, too, in the opposite direction.

Bruce grunted and made a lunge for the cat.

Rascal leaped from the shelf.

And landed on me.

Darkness enveloped us as Rascal's back feet caught the rail, pulling down clothes on top of him and me, and knocking me to the floor.

Rascal wriggled out from under the clothes and ran a short distance away shaking himself off.

Jac skidded around the room door. "There you are," she said to the cat. "What happened?" she asked as she saw the mess.

Bruce pointed to the cat. "He happened."

Jac picked up Rascal, who purred in contentment. "Oh no. Rascal, you bad boy."

"Watch the door while we clean up," Bruce said as he uncovered me and helped me to stand.

Together we sorted and hung up the clothes.

As I shook out the last article of clothing, a coat, I heard a crinkling sound from one of the pockets. "Found something."

Bruce extracted a piece of paper from the pocket.

"What is it?" I asked as I peeked over Bruce's arm to read.

"I'm not sure."

Sirens shrieked close by.

Bruce cocked his head at the sound. "Hang up that coat."

I ignored his command in favor of reading the paper. "She said she had no idea he was going to be here."

Jac asked from the doorway, "She who? He who?"

"Karen," I answered as I continued to scan the paper. "This is a letter with her name at the top. Demanding she meet with Cafferty here. It's signed by him."

Bruce turned the paper over to reveal a blank side. "If that's Cafferty's signature."

Jac tightened her hold on Rascal who wiggled to get down. "That's all it says?"

"Yes. Cafferty threatens to expose her secret if she doesn't show up."

I checked the pockets of the coat I held. Nothing.

Sirens shrieked right outside then stopped. Uncle Harry was here.

Bruce folded the paper and shoved it into the coat pocket. "Hang it up."

I did, as he turned to Jac. "Better get downstairs."

Jac hesitated. "Did you find Robert?"

"Yes," I said. "He took Pedro home."

Jac's breath whooshed out, and she swept out the door with Rascal in her arms, the cat's tail twitching back and forth.

"You're leaving the evidence? How will we determine if the letter is from Cafferty without keeping it?"

Bruce stripped off his gloves and motioned for me to do the same. "I'll make sure Harry compares the signature to the registration book. William has one, right?"

I removed my gloves and handed them to Bruce. "I have no idea. He may check guests in with a computer, but there should be some record of a signature. Jac will know though."

Downstairs Harry's commanding voice boomed. "Where is everyone?"

William's voice was too low for me to hear his reply.

"Heldman, stay with the guests. Where's the body?"

Harry's heavy tread mounted the stairs. He wasn't alone by the sound of the footsteps.

Bruce and I stepped into the hall to wait. Bruce hid the latex gloves in his pants pockets.

Harry topped the stairs with two officers behind him and turned toward us, his long steps striding down the hall. He stopped by us and glanced into the room. With a grimace, he motioned for the other two men to enter the room.

"What happened?" Harry adjusted the volume of his radio on his belt. The police chatter quieted.

"Madeline Wells is dead." Bruce pointed to the bed. "We believe she was smothered with a pillow."

Harry raised his eyebrows. "Show me."

Bruce stepped into the room and pointed to the pillow.

Harry stripped on gloves and examined the pillow. "Bag it," he said to Officer Barnes.

"Where were the guests when Ms. Taylor found the body?"

"Most were sleeping as far as we know. Except for Karen Taylor. She was outside."

Harry jerked his head up to stare at Bruce. "How do you know that?"

"I was patrolling outside when Paw alerted me to her." Bruce explained his encounter with Karen and how he met Patricia and me in the kitchen.

Harry glared at me. "What were you doing here?"

"Bruce suggested we stay the night in hopes of preventing the killer from attacking."

Bruce grimaced as he glanced at Madeline. "I failed."

"You can't blame yourself." I touched his arm, but he jerked away.

"She's right," Harry said as he pulled latex gloves from his pocket and handed them to Bruce. "Now. What did you find when you searched the room?"

My eyes widened. Before I could deny anything, Harry held up a hand. "I know you two. It'll save me some time if you point out what you found."

I accepted a pair of gloves from Officer Barnes and showed Harry the fake gun. As he examined it, I explained, "It's a prop for the murder mystery game we planned to play this weekend. Hans Greble carved weapons to use as clues for the game. Shelbee hid them around the B&B for the players to find."

"How did it get here?"

I shrugged.

Harry grunted. "Anything else?"

I directed him to the closet and showed him the paper in the coat pocket, explaining how Rascal knocked the clothes down.

Harry unfolded the letter and scrunched his brow as he read. "Barnes, go find out if Innsman has a register the guests sign or a sample of Cafferty's signature. If so, bring it up here."

"Yes, sir."

Officer Barnes strode away.

"I'll be back in a minute," Harry said to Officer Banks, who was documenting the scene.

The officer nodded as he continued his work.

Harry waved us out of the room and halfway down the hall. He stopped and said to Bruce, "What did you find out?"

"Nothing yet. I'm waiting for my sources to return my calls."

I crossed my arms. "Sources?"

"Informants. I sent out inquiries about our victim's and suspect's pasts."

My voice edged with anger. "When were you going to tell me?"

Bruce scowled. "As soon as I learned anything."

Harry put a hand on each of our shoulders. "Easy you two. Let's—"

Crash!

CHAPTER 17

Loud, angry voices followed the sound of the something breaking downstairs.

Harry bolted down the hall.

"Boss?" The officer documenting Madeline's room stepped into the hall.

Harry waved, calling over his shoulder, "Keep working. I'll handle this."

Bruce sprinted past Harry and took the stairs two at a time, Harry right behind him.

I rushed down the stairs and skidded into Jac, who ran in from the kitchen hall.

We hurried to the living room door, stopping short of entering the packed room.

James stood, arm raised, threatening Jessica with a chair leg, the broken chair smashed at his feet.

Officers Heldman and Barnes faced James, their guns

trained on him.

Harry stood between his officers attempting to reason with James. “Put down the weapon, Mr. Dayton. Step away from Ms. St. Clair.”

“No way. She's been spreading lies about me. Insinuating that I killed Cafferty and now that woman.” He raised the chair leg higher.

William and Patricia struggled to hold Donna back, as she cursed her husband. “Stop this nonsense, James. You're acting like a brute.”

James ignored her, jerking his attention between Jessica and Harry.

From the corner of my left eye, I caught movement. A slight shift of my head and I saw Bruce edging around the room to get behind James.

Suddenly the dogs ran past us into the living room.

“Woof!”

“Growl!”

“Yip. Yip.”

“Woo-woo.”

“Rats!” Jac said low enough that only I could hear. “I forgot to shut the door.”

Paw forced his way between Harry and the officer on his right while Samuel ran behind the sofa.

Paw slammed into James's chest as Samuel clamped onto the chair leg, ripping it from James's hand.

James landed on his back with an “oomph.” Paw pinned him to the floor, lying across the man’s chest.

Samuel lay down and chewed on the chair leg.

Henry walked around James and lifted his leg.

"No!" Patricia and William yelled as James turned his head to avoid a stream of urine in his face.

Shelbee stifled a giggle as she knelt by Samuel, coaxing him to release the weapon he chewed on.

I held a hand to my chest, my heart beating rapidly. I was thankful both officers had maintained control of their weapons when Paw pushed through them.

Harry took charge. "Clarissa, call off Paw."

"Paw, come here!"

Paw leaped up and trotted to me, tail waving.

Harry pointed at James. "Get him up and cuff him."

The officers obeyed, warily watching Henry and Bitsy, who sniffed James's shoes.

Shelbee retrieved the chair leg from Samuel and handed it to Harry, who shook drool off his hand.

Jac picked up Bitsy as she cavorted past her.

Donna wrenched from William and Patricia's hold, hurried to James, and slapped him. "You idiot. What were you thinking?"

"She's a liar!"

"Yes, she is, but you can't threaten people."

"No. You can't." Harry motioned to his officers. "Take him down to the station."

"I'm coming too." Donna glared at Harry as if challenging him to contradict her.

"Fine." Harry clenched his jaw.

The front door clicked as someone opened it then again as it was closed.

"Woof!" Paw's bark was joyous.

I peeked out of the living room and smiled.

Hal was back. His fierce scowl softened when he saw me. "At least I'm not the only one Harry called out at this hour."

Donna spoke behind me. "We need to dress. We're still in our pajamas."

I turned to face the room while Paw greeted Hal, who stroked my dog's back.

Harry grumbled to himself and then said, "All right. My officers will escort you upstairs and stay while you change clothes."

"No way." Donna fisted her hands on her hips. "I'm not undressing in front of one of them." She nodded to the officers.

"Then you'll go in the clothes you're wearing."

I cleared my throat. "Why don't I stay with Donna as she changes?" Before Harry protested, I added, "Heldman and Barnes can go in the Daytons' room while James changes then they can stand outside the door as I go in while Donna changes."

Patricia touched Harry's arm for his attention. "It's too chilly for them to go in their nightclothes. I'll accompany Clarissa to help Donna."

Harry scanned the room. "All right. Bruce, you stay here. No conversing amongst yourselves. We'll be conducting interviews soon."

He motioned to his men. "Take them upstairs."

Jac and I stepped back to let the officers and James

through the door. Donna followed, pulling her robe tighter around her.

Harry nodded to us as he passed and waved for Hal to follow.

Patricia stopped next to me. "Are you bringing Paw?"

I smiled at my dog as he stared up with a hopeful expression. "Yes."

Behind us, Bruce said, "Everybody, sit back down. We'll wait in silence until the Chief returns."

Jessica, who had remained subdued during James's threat, complained, "He's the troublemaker. I bet he killed that woman. Why do we have to sit and wait?"

Karen sobbed. "You're horrible. 'That woman,' as you call her, was my friend. And she was a kind and caring person."

"I just bet."

"Why you-"

"Ladies," Bruce spoke in exasperation. "No talking."

The room fell silent.

Patricia and I climbed the stairs behind Harry and Hal, who headed down the hall and turned into Madeline's room.

Directly across the hall, Donna waited by her door as the officers led James into the Daytons' room.

Paw sniffed a trail along the hall as Patricia and I walked to Donna's side.

Donna, who was leaning forward to glance in Madeline's room, asked, "How did she die?"

"I don't know." I lied hoping Karen wouldn't reveal

the truth until Harry released the information.

I peeked into the room. Hal stood by Madeline's body, examining her.

Harry peered around the door at us, scowled, and slammed the door.

"How rude." Donna hugged herself.

Paw sniffed the bottom of Madeline's door and across to Donna's. Satisfied, he flopped down in front of her door.

Patricia smiled at Paw but spoke to Donna. "The Chief conducts his investigations with utmost discretion."

Donna shivered. "What if the killer had chosen our room instead? James and I could be dead."

"You're assuming a random killer is on the loose?" Patricia sounded affronted. "I assure you our inn is a safe place."

"Doesn't look like it." Donna sniped back.

"Perhaps it is connected to Cafferty's death," I said as I tightened the sash of my robe.

"Cafferty." Donna glowered. "That vile man. He deserved to die."

She saw our shocked faces and amended her words. "Never mind me. I'm tired and worried about James."

I nodded. "Understandable."

The door opened, and Officer Heldman stopped short when he encountered Paw at his feet.

I grabbed Paw's collar and urged him to stand.

He got up and we stepped back.

The officer led James out of the room.

Barnes followed and stepped next to the door frame. "I'll wait here for you."

Heldman escorted James down the hall and descended the stairs.

Donna and Patricia entered the room, and I followed with Paw.

I closed the door behind me with a click.

Paw trailed a scent around the room as Donna selected a pair of pants and a sweater from the closet.

A full-size bed dominated the room. Nightstands bookended the bed with a lamp on each. The lamp closest to the door was lit. A dresser stood to the right of the door, on it a profusion of lotions, discarded jewelry, and a handbag. Across from the bed, the closet door stood ajar. It was packed with clothing, most of which appeared to be Donna's.

I preferred to travel light with a bag or two. Donna must have brought six suitcases to carry all her clothes.

She sat on the lone chair in the room that was centered between the closet and one of two windows. Both windows faced the street in front of the house.

I scanned the room. There was no sign of James's habitation.

Donna sighed. "That feels better. I hated wearing my nightclothes with those men around."

I assumed she meant the officers.

Patricia sat on the bed. "They are good men. They wouldn't harm you."

"They arrested James."

"He shouldn't have threatened Jessica," Patricia reminded her.

Donna crossed her arms. "Jessica is a liar. She's accusing us of murder. Yet no one questions her past. She's not innocent you know."

Paw tracked a scent past Patricia back toward me.

"What do you mean?" I asked Donna.

"You should ask Jessica about her past. It wasn't only Cafferty she knew before this weekend."

"Who did she know? Madeline?"

Donna pursed her mouth. "That's for you to find out. I won't cast aspersions like she's doing."

I thought she already was but refrained from commenting.

Crash!

I jumped and jerked my head to the right as Donna screamed, "Bad dog!"

Behind me, Officer Barnes knocked on the door. "Everything all right?"

Donna ran across the room where Paw stood with his head shoved into a handbag. The same handbag that he had pulled off the dresser. The contents were scattered around Paw's feet.

The officer knocked louder. "I'm coming in!"

The door bumped into my back as Barnes opened it.

Donna crouched next to Paw frantically gathering her spilled possessions. "Get your mangy mutt away from my things."

"He's not mangy!"

Patricia knelt by Donna, picking up a hairbrush and lipstick. She glanced at me and nodded her head to Paw with a scowl.

"Best get him out of here," Officer Barnes said to me.

I walked over and grabbed Paw's collar using my free hand to detach the purse. Paw was wedged so tightly the purse wouldn't budge.

Barnes knelt by me and pulled the purse off Paw. My dog's head freed from the purse with a pop.

Drool coated Barnes's hands and the inside of Donna's handbag.

"Yuck!" Donna said as she cradled her belongings. A wallet, glasses, and scarf were clutched in her hands.

Paw shook his head sending more drool flying. Donna sat back on her heels to avoid it, but she got hit as did the rest of us.

"That dog is a menace. Now I have to change again." She stood up and dropped her things on the chair by the closet. She turned to the officer with hands on hips and stared pointedly at the door.

Patricia gathered up the rest of her things and retrieved the bag. "Clarissa, why don't you and Officer Barnes wait outside with Paw?"

I sighed, stood up, and tugged Paw's collar. I turned to Donna. "My apologies. I'll pay to replace anything damaged."

Donna glared but nodded with a quick jerk.

I guided Paw out with Barnes behind me.

He closed the door with a huge grin on his face. In a whisper, he said, "It's always fun when Paw's around." Apparently, Barnes wasn't bothered by the drool stuck to his uniform.

I knelt by Paw who dropped an object at my feet.

Big, brown eyes stared at me in anticipation of praise.

I reached out to pick up the object. A pen. It was gold-colored with a dull metallic sheen from the hall lights reflecting off it.

"Wait!" Barnes commanded me as he removed a plastic glove from his belt pouch. "The drool."

He pulled on the latex glove and bent to retrieve the pen.

Paw issued a querying, "Woof," as Barnes stood up. The pen dripped drool onto the hall carpet.

I rubbed Paw's chest. "Let Officer Barnes have it."

Barnes examined the pen as I considered how to reprimand Paw.

Before I could say anything, Donna opened the door and stepped out. Patricia followed close behind.

Donna gazed at us with a curious expression.

"Ma'am? Does this pen belong to you?" The officer held it up for her to see.

Donna shrank back from the drool-coated pen. "Yuck!"

Patricia spoke in an amused voice, "Perhaps you should wipe it off first, Officer."

Paw watched with his head tilted on the side.

Barnes wiped off as much drool as he could with his glove. He held the pen up for Donna's inspection.

"Woof!" Paw stepped forward, reluctant to see his prize returned.

Donna peered at the pen and paled. "That's not mine." She took a step back but had to stop retreating, for Patricia stood at her back.

A commotion on the stairs drew our attention, and we swiveled in that direction. All except Paw, whose gaze remained fixed on the pen.

Bruce, who had remained with the guests in the living room, ordered, "Ms. St. Clair, come back here."

"No. I'm going to put on clothes."

Light footsteps tapped up the stairs followed by heavy footfalls.

Jessica topped the stairs, nightgown swishing around her, and swiveled to speak to her pursuer. She stopped in mid-turn as she caught sight of us.

Gesturing to Donna, Jessica said, "She changed clothes." Jessica flitted down the hall toward us as the door to Madeline's room opened.

Harry stepped out behind me. "What's going on here?"

Bruce said as he topped the stairs, pointing to Jessica, "She refused to stay with the others."

Jessica continued toward us, saying, "I won't sit around in my nightclothes waiting for you." She glowered at Harry then turned to Donna.

"She," Jessica pointed to Donna and gasped. "That's Thomas's pen."

CHAPTER 18

Harry's voice rumbled behind me. "What pen?"

Officer Barnes held up the pen. "This, sir." He nodded to Paw and gestured to Donna. "He found it in her purse."

"Impossible. I've never seen that pen before now."

Jessica planted her fists on her hips. "Then how did it get in your purse?"

"You can't prove it was in my purse." She flung a hand toward Paw. "He could have found it somewhere else."

I huffed. "Not true!"

Harry placed a firm hand on my shoulder. "Let me see that pen."

Barnes handed it to Harry, who wore plastic gloves from his search of Madeline's room. As Harry raised it to the light to examine it, I saw an inscription down the pen's length. *Thomas Cafferty*.

Hal stepped out of Madeline's room. "I'm ready to move her."

Harry grunted and handed the pen back to his officer. "Bag it."

Hal shook his head. "What kind of arrogant idiot has their name engraved on a pen?" Obviously, he, too, had seen the inscription as Harry held the pen.

Jessica glared at Hal, but Harry spoke before she could chastise the coroner. "I want a full explanation of how Paw found the pen." He turned to Jessica. "Are you willing to swear that pen was Cafferty's?"

She lifted her chin. "Yes."

Harry nodded with a jerk of his head. "Fine. Go get dressed. Patricia, go with her, then I want to talk to you. Don't discuss the pen or how it was found."

Jessica huffed. "I'll dress alone."

"No. You won't. Once you're done, you'll go to the police station with the Daytons." He turned to Donna. "You're going to the station. Consider yourself a person of interest."

Donna crossed her arms. "And if I refuse?"

"I'll detain you for suspected theft."

Donna scoffed. "You can't do that."

"Try me."

Donna flounced away saying, "I'm calling my lawyer." She brushed past Jessica and Bruce.

Officer Barnes followed her.

Patricia gestured to Jessica. "Let's go, dear."

"I'm not your dear." Jessica turned on her heel and headed to her room. Once both women were ensconced in Jessica's room, Harry said, "Bruce go back to the other guests."

Bruce nodded to Harry and smiled at me. He walked down the hall and disappeared down the steps.

Hal scratched Paw's back. "Good boy. You're a better detective than Harry."

Harry grunted. "He'd make a better coroner too."

"You ready for me to move the body?"

"Yeah."

Hal returned to the room.

Harry took my arm and led me downstairs.

Paw trotted along beside us.

As we walked, he said, "I'm going down to the station. Tell Bruce to keep everyone in the living room until I send an officer back. Banks will finish upstairs."

He paused at the bottom of the stairs and directed me to the dining room.

Once inside he pulled out a chair for me. "Now tell me what happened in Mrs. Dayton's room."

I sat down, and Paw settled at my feet. I recounted how he stuck his head in Donna's purse, spilling the contents.

Harry shook his head. "That dog *is* a better detective. He gets away with unruly behavior."

"Woof!" It sounded like a protest to me.

"Uncle, we're fortunate he found the pen."

"Maybe." Harry scratched his stubble-coated jaw. "Maybe not. The pen may have no connection to the murders."

"So you believe Cafferty's death was murder."

Harry nodded.

Voices in the foyer drew Harry's attention.

"Stop following me," Jessica sharp voice complained.

Patricia's soothing voice was too low for me to hear the words she spoke.

Harry stood up. "I'll talk with you later."

He left the dining room and spoke to Jessica. "Come with me, Ms. St. Clair."

"Why do I have to go anywhere?"

"Because I need your statement regarding the pen. Besides, if you want to press charges against Mr. Dayton, I need you to come to the station."

"Fine," she huffed.

High heels clicked across the floor as Harry opened the front door. Through the dining room door, I glimpsed Jessica step out, followed by Harry.

"Come on, boy." I stood up.

Paw sighed and got to his feet.

We crossed the foyer to the living room.

Above, I heard sounds of movement. Hal must be bringing down Madeline's body.

I shuddered. I didn't wish to see them, so I closed the living room door behind me. Everyone stared at me.

"They're moving her."

Karen sobbed quietly, and I mentally kicked myself for upsetting her.

Patricia sat beside William with Henry nestled at their feet.

Shelbee sat on one sofa with a comforting arm around Karen's shoulders.

Jac sat on the floor between Samuel and Henry while Bruce paced by the windows.

Bitsy curled up next to Shelbee on the sofa cushion.

Paw joined Samuel. I approached Bruce. Quietly I said, "Harry wants you to keep everyone here until he sends an officer."

Bruce nodded curtly then hugged me. He whispered in my ear, "You okay?"

I whispered back. "Yes, but I wish I knew who the murderer is."

Bruce kissed my forehead. "Me too. We'll figure it out."

Clattering sounded in the foyer.

I sensed the tension rise in the room.

Bruce squeezed me then strode to the door and slipped out, closing it behind him.

I sat on the sofa across from Shelbee and Karen and stared at the abandoned tea tray. "Would anyone like some fresh tea or coffee?"

Karen shook her head, declining my offer, but Shelbee said, "Bring hot tea with sugar." She nodded to Karen.

I stood up, lifting the tray of now cold beverages. "Anyone else?"

William coughed. "I'll have coffee."

"Me too," Patricia said. "Can I help you prepare it?"

"No. I'll get it." As I turned the doorknob, Paw brushed against me. He wasn't letting me out of his sight.

"Okay, boy, you can come too."

I planned to prepare the tea in the commercial kitchen. As we neared the door to the family's private kitchen, Paw stuck his head through the gap in the door. I followed Paw inside planning to give him a treat. The dogs' biscuit tin sat on the counter.

I grabbed the tin, prying off the top when a rapping sound startled me. I jerked, and biscuits flew everywhere.

Paw greeted this sudden good fortune with a woof and a dash to eat as many as he could.

I rushed around, grabbing up as many biscuits as I could while calling, "just a minute," toward the outer door.

Fortunately, most of the treats landed on the counter. I swept them into the tin and corralled the remaining treats on the floor.

Paw stood over three more biscuits, so I let him have them and hurried to the kitchen door. I paused before opening it. "Who is it?"

"Well for goodness' sakes, do you think the killer would knock?" Lillian asked through the door.

"Now Lillian," Mark Carter's voice admonished.

"Don't now Lillian me, young man."

I pulled open the door and stepped back.

Lillian hustled in with Mark on her heels. Robert followed, shaking his head at his two companions.

"What are you all doing here?" I asked with hands on hips.

"What do you think?" Lillian groused. "I came for the mystery game, but this one," she pointed to Mark, "says there's been another murder."

I opened my mouth to ask Mark how he knew someone had been killed then shook my head. "The sirens."

"Yep." Mark pulled out his notebook and pen. "Not often our police force uses their sirens. Twice in two days. Had to be something big. So, who died?"

"Mark," Robert placed a hand on the other man's shoulder, "give her a minute. You don't have to push so hard."

I expected our resident reporter to bristle at Robert's advice, but he merely shrugged, saying, "Someone has to find out the truth."

Paw finished his snack and sniffed Lillian's shoes. She peered at him. "Saber isn't with me, you big galoot." Her tone was affectionate.

Paw sat down and gazed up at her, his head tilted to the side.

"He's sleeping at my house," Lillian informed Paw.

I stifled a smile for I knew Lillian wouldn't appreciate my amusement at her conversation with Paw. I glanced over to Robert, whose eyes twinkled in mischief.

I turned to the door to cross into the commercial kitchen and start the tea.

Mark was missing.

"Drat that man! Where did he go?"

Robert strode to the door, saying, "I'll find him."

I followed but stopped when Lillian said, "Where are you going?"

"To the other kitchen to prepare tea. Would you like some?"

"Tell me what happened. Who's dead?" Lillian followed me, as did Paw.

"Sorry, boy. You're not allowed in the other kitchen. Wait here and I'll let you out as soon as I've finished the tea."

I placed my hands on his chest and urged him to stay back. He stared at me with sad eyes as I slipped out the door with Lillian.

In the kitchen, I boiled water as Lillian fixed a tray with cups, spoons, and sugar. I turned from the stove to find Lillian standing with arms crossed.

"Madeline Wells died. Smothered with a bed pillow."

"Hmm. Wouldn't have expected that although she did seem a nosy person."

"Nosy?" I asked as I searched the cupboard for cookies.

"She wanted Cafferty's clues."

"His clues?"

"Yes," Lillian said, throwing her hands in the air. "Last

night when you all voted on continuing the mystery game. Madeline wanted Cafferty's clues."

"She did. Maybe she's just competitive."

"That too, but I think she was nosy as well."

Shelbee pushed through the door. "Mark is a pain in the you-know-what. But Officer Heldman is back and ordered him to shut up and wait until we're interviewed." She poured hot water into the teapot then turned to me. "He says you are free to do what you want. Harry's orders are for you to stay out of it."

I frowned.

"If I were you," Shelbee said," I'd go out the back to avoid Mark. He's waiting to ask you questions since you're the only one released."

Lillian stood up and pushed in her chair. "Let's go."

"Go where?" I asked.

"To talk to Dana."

Lillian hadn't forgotten about the missing bracelet.

"All right. We'll take Paw."

"Samuel's in the there too." Shelbee lifted the tray. "Take him along."

I opened the door for her to pass by me then Lillian and I crossed into the private kitchen. Paw and Samuel greeted us with wagging tails.

I grabbed Jac's coat off a hook since mine was upstairs. "We'll stop at my house first, so I can change out of my nightclothes." It would be chilly with my pajamas on, but it was a short drive to my house. Jac's car keys were in the pocket of her coat, and I knew she wouldn't mind me driving her car.

"Lillian, how did you get here? You didn't walk, did you?"

She shrugged. "I started walking, but Robert stopped and picked me up. Don't frown at me. I may be old, but I'm fit." She poked my side. "Fitter than you."

I refrained from arguing, partly because she was right. I snapped on Paw and Samuel's leashes. "Let's go."

I drove to my house, changed clothes, and drove out of town to the hiking trails. Samuel and Paw shared the back seat to Paw's displeasure. He usually rode in the front seat.

According to Lillian, Dana Harford jogged the hiking trail through Cotter's Woods every day. Cotter's Woods was owned by Daniel Winter, our local taxidermist. Odd to think a taxidermist would have a deep respect for nature but he did. Cotter's Woods was as much a nature preserve as a hiking trail. It was open to the public if people didn't litter or harm the animals and woods.

I passed the development where Robert lived and turned down a two-lane dirt road. The road wound uphill to the woods. Once I crested the hill, a graded parking lot spread out. A few cars sat in the lot, and I parked next to a red Toyota.

Lillian pointed to the red car. "That's Dana's."

I gazed at the woods where the main trail led into the trees and wondered how we were going to find Dana in there.

Lillian glanced at her watch. "Perfect timing. Dana should be just nearing the fairy house. If we take the trail to the right a short distance, we can wait by the first bench. She should jog past in five minutes."

I marveled at Lillian's knowledge. "Have you spied on her?"

Lillian waved a hand, dismissing my question. "Of course not. Terry Wilkes volunteers up here. He patrols the trails and clears dead wood. That type of thing. He knows all the regulars and their schedules."

I shook my head at the silent spy network. Tranquil Valley had more secrets than I ever knew.

We climbed out of the car, and the dogs and I followed Lillian to the bench she indicated.

Paw and Samuel sniffed around the bench. A squirrel in a tree branch overhead chattered at us.

"Grr." Samuel bristled at the squirrel's rude remarks.

I placed a hand on his head. "Ignore him."

Samuel whined and sat down, watching his furry tormenter.

Paw trailed a scent around the bench then sighed and sat down on my other side.

The fairy house wasn't visible from here, but I thought of how beautiful it looked last Christmas.

It was named because of its tiny size and resembled the cottage the dwarfs lived in in the *Snow White* stories. Only two people could fit in the house at a time though. Kids loved to explore it and the town paid to decorate it each year for the holidays. Someone had figured out how to run the white lights it was decorated with by battery.

As I mused, a tall, thin woman wearing a red sweat suit jogged into view.

Lillian stepped onto the trail blocking the path.

The woman pulled up in surprise. “Mrs. Hardcastle. What are you doing here?”

CHAPTER 19

She glanced over at the dogs and me. Her mouth pinched as Paw and Samuel stood up.

I tightened my grip on the leashes. "They are well-behaved."

Dana nodded.

Lillian stepped close to the woman. "I have some questions for you."

I groaned. Lillian wasn't approaching this subtly. To my surprise, Dana dropped her gaze to the ground.

"What questions?" she mumbled.

"You know very well what questions." Lillian crossed her arms. "Why is Joan lying about losing her bracelet?"

Dana lifted her chin in defiance. "What business is it of yours?"

Lillian shook a finger in the woman's face. "It became

my business when that bracelet ended up around my cat's neck."

I guessed Dana's age to be mid-fifties and yet she was cowed by Lillian. "I'm sorry Saber got involved. Is he okay?"

Lillian's expression softened. "He's fine. Thank you for asking. Now, why is Joan lying?"

Dana shifted from foot to foot. "She wanted to punish Cal."

Lillian hmphed. "Why would Joan want to punish her husband?"

Dana pushed up her sweatshirt sleeves. "He gave Joan the bracelet for her birthday."

"So?"

"She discovered at the hairdresser that he gave a more expensive necklace to his secretary. Carla was getting her hair done, too, and she was bragging about it. Joan was furious. She met me in the park afterwards and claimed if he didn't love her enough to give her the more expensive gift then she wasn't keeping it. She was so mad that she dropped it in the flower bed by the gazebo and scraped mulch over it. Later, she found out that Carla lied. The necklace was a fake one, and Cal hadn't given it to her. She'd bought it herself to make David Kemple jealous."

Paw lay down next to me, sighing as if to say humans were confusing.

I agreed.

Dana shrugged. "She went back to get it, but it was gone."

Lillian snorted. "It seems she got what she deserved. Why didn't she admit it?"

"She didn't want Cal to find out. Please, Lillian, you can't tell Cal about this. Joan would be furious with me."

"Joan's an idiot."

Samuel whined, restless to be moving. He nudged Paw who stood up and shook himself.

"Dana," I said, "we'll keep Joan's secret. I'll speak with Uncle Harry and inform him that the bracelet belongs to Joan."

Both Dana and Lillian began to protest.

I raised my hand to forestall them. "No crime was committed. The bracelet is at Seth's jewelry store."

Dana gasped. "That's where Cal bought it."

Lillian grumbled. "No crime. Saber could have been injured with that bracelet around his neck."

"I know Lillian, but Joan didn't put it on him. Perhaps you could speak with Joan about donating to one of the animal charities."

I nodded to Dana. "Tell Joan she can pick up her bracelet from Seth. With luck, he won't have called Cal yet."

"I'll do that right now." Dana turned to Lillian. "I'll suggest a donation to Joan. If she won't do it, I will."

Lillian nodded once, and Dana jogged past us.

Pursing her lips, Lillian grumbled, "Joan needs her backside kicked."

I touched her shoulder. "She lied, but she didn't

commit a crime. Kara is the one who put the collar on Saber."

"I know that," Lillian said. "I can't blame the dear girl either."

I smiled. "Lillian, I think you are a softy under that hard exterior."

She hmphed.

A squirrel scampered onto the trail, and Samuel jumped up, lunging at it.

I tightened my grip, feeling pain in my shoulder.

Lillian pulled two dog treats from her pocket and waved one in front of Samuel.

The squirrel scampered into the trees. Samuel continued to strain at the leash until Paw nudged him as he took one of the treats. Samuel sighed and accepted the other dog biscuit.

I released my breath. Thank goodness Samuel relaxed at Paw's actions.

"Come on," I said. "I've got to find Harry and tell him to release the bracelet."

"And we've got a killer to catch."

I stumbled at her words. "We?"

Lillian raised an eyebrow. "Of course, we. You didn't think I'd leave you to face a killer alone."

I thought about how to dissuade Lillian. No easy feat.

As we drove back to town, I racked my brain for a way to convince Lillian to go home. She was a stubborn woman, and every idea I thought of was quickly dismissed.

I stopped at the police station and went in to speak to Harry. If anyone could change Lillian's mind, it would be him. But the desk officer informed me Harry was unavailable. I left a note for my uncle telling him about the bracelet and asking him to tell Seth to release it to Joan.

I returned to the car and drove to the B&B. As I accelerated up the hill and turned right into the inn's parking lot, I glimpsed Henry trotting down the sidewalk with Patricia and William. I stopped the car and Lillian rolled down her window.

"Are the officers finished?"

William bent down to the window. "They are with us. Bruce was talking with Officer Heldman when we left."

Patricia leaned down and began to speak, but Henry woofed, interrupting her.

Paw and Samuel pushed up behind Lillian's seat. "Woof! Ruff!"

"Paw! Stop that!" I put the car in park and turned in my seat, grabbing his collar. I pulled him back as Lillian covered her ears, complaining, "Noisy mutts."

"Samuel! Paw! Quiet!"

William fussed at Henry.

The dogs quieted, and Paw sat down with a sheepish look on his face.

I turned back to face the open window. "Sorry. What were you saying, Patricia?"

"Shelbee and Jac offered to clean up after we served a buffet breakfast. Karen ate and then went out. Her room is cordoned off, and she said she couldn't face entering that room again."

"I can't blame her. Did she say where she was going?"

Patricia flexed the hand holding Henry's leash. "She didn't say, but I'd be surprised if she willingly stayed with us tonight."

Lillian pet Henry as he stood up against the car. "Can you offer her another room?"

"Maybe." Patricia tilted her head at me. "If Robert doesn't mind moving?"

"I'll ask him," I said as I put the car in drive. "See you later."

They waved as we drove through the lot to park near the back.

Lillian rolled up her window. "Would you stay in Karen's old room?"

I shuddered. "Not a chance."

I parked near the walk leading to the kitchen.

The dogs jumped out of the car after Lillian.

Shelbee and Jac were strolling toward us as we rounded the corner of the house.

Bitsy pranced along behind Shelbee.

Paw growled low in his throat at the sight of the little dog, but Samuel padded over and nudged her with his nose. She sniffed at his feet and danced on her hind legs, delighted to see him.

Paw whined, and I pulled him close to me.

"We're going for groceries," Shelbee said as she scratched Samuel's back.

Jac picked up Bitsy, motioning to the Pomeranian. "Figured she could use some attention and a walk."

"Is Robert or Mark still here?"

"No," Jac said. "Bruce told Mark to leave. Mark argued, of course, but the officers came in and ordered him to go."

"And Robert went to the theater since the mystery game was canceled. He said if we need him we're to call." Shelbee took Samuel's leash from me. She nodded to the house. "Bruce is the only one left."

"Okay," I said. "We'll go see him. Oh, by the way, do you think Robert will trade rooms with Karen?"

Jac scrunched up her face. "I'm not sure the police are finished yet."

"They're still collecting evidence?"

"No," Shelbee said. "But it's cordoned off, and Officer Heldman forbade anyone from entering the room. He wouldn't say when Karen could go back in. She wept when he told her."

Jac nodded. "And she's left the B&B. We don't know where she went."

"Patricia mentioned it. Harry will want to know about that."

"Bruce told Officer Heldman and he informed Harry." Shelbee chucked Bitsy under her chin. "We'll see you later."

Lillian stared after them as they disappeared around the side of the house. "Why doesn't Paw like the little dog? What do you call her? Bitsy?"

Paw whined.

"It's a long story. You remember the Englishes who used to live next door to me?"

She nodded.

"They had a Pom like Bitsy who barked and bit at Paw when he was a puppy. One day she leaped out of the bushes at Paw and landed on his back, scrabbling with her claws. Paw's hated Poms ever since then. Some he tolerates better than others. He's better with Bitsy now than when they first met, but it's slow going."

"How can you tell them apart? Don't all Poms look the same?"

"Don't all black cats?" I retorted, reminding her of Saber.

"Of course not!"

We entered through the personal kitchen door and walked to the foyer. Bruce stood by the front door shaking Officer Heldman's hand. Heldman inclined his head to Lillian and me and left. Bruce closed the door and crossed his arms. "How did it go?"

"That's what we want to know." Lillian copied Bruce's stance with arms crossed.

"We spoke with Dana. Joan is the one who buried her bracelet." I unhooked Paw's leash since he was straining to greet Bruce.

Paw ran over to him, tail wagging.

Bruce scratched Paw's head, saying, "Hey, big guy." He looked up at me. "Why?"

Lillian answered. "Because she's a ninny. Let's sit

down." She led the way to the living room and sat on the sofa facing the windows.

I sat next to Lillian. "Joan was mad at Cal."

Bruce took the opposite sofa with Paw, who stretched out with his head on Bruce's leg. "Cal?"

"Her husband. Apparently, his secretary bragged that he had given her an expensive gift. Joan felt slighted and threw the bracelet he'd given her away, burying it at the gazebo."

Lillian snorted. "She's an idiot."

I ignored her. "She went to retrieve it after she discovered the secretary lied, but by then Saber had found it and Kara put it on him as a collar."

"You told Harry?" Bruce caressed Paw's shoulders. My Saint wore a blissful expression.

"He wasn't available when I stopped at the station, but I left him a note to ask Seth to turn over the bracelet to Joan. I suppose I could talk to Seth myself."

"Don't bother," Bruce said. "Seth won't do anything without Harry's approval."

Lillian fidgeted in her seat. "What happened while we were gone?"

Bruce scratched his jaw. He'd changed clothes but hadn't shaven. Dark stubble bristled on his face. "Mark Carter showed up and badgered me for information. I argued with him until Harry's officers arrived. They sent him away with a statement."

My stomach growled, and I blushed. "What about Karen?"

Bruce grunted. “You need some breakfast. Shelbee and Jac set out a buffet.”

“Let's eat,” Lillian said as she stood up.

Paw lifted his head at the mention of food. “Woof.” He sat up, jumped off the sofa, and led the way to the commercial kitchen.

I grabbed his collar. “You can't go in there. No dogs allowed.”

He whined.

“I'll take him.” Bruce held Paw back. “We'll wait for you in the other kitchen.”

I nodded and ushered Lillian to the food.

“I wondered why they had two kitchens,” Lillian mumbled to herself. “Seems silly to me.”

“I know, but the health department has strict rules. Besides, some guests don't like pets.”

“Fools, if you ask me,” Lillian said as she selected a slice of toast.

We loaded our plates and crossed the hall to join Bruce and Paw.

Paw crunched on his kibble, lifting his head to watch us sit at the table.

We ate in silence for a few minutes until Lillian waved at Bruce. “Tell us the rest.”

“Karen was questioned first and then she left. She refuses to go back to her old room. The police wouldn't let her move her stuff.”

“Shelbee told us the room is cordoned off,” I said before taking a bite of eggs.

Bruce nodded. "It is. Heldman questioned the rest of us. William and Patricia left with Henry after giving their statements."

"We met them as we returned." Lillian drank her coffee. "Where's Rascal?"

"The cat?" Bruce shrugged. "In Patricia and William's apartment, I think."

"Hasn't anyone checked on the dear boy?" Lillian set down her mug and pushed back her chair. "I'm going up to check on him."

Bruce protested. "I can't let you go into the Innsman's room."

Lillian faced Bruce with hands on hips. "Then go with me. But I am checking on him."

I put my hand on Bruce's arm. "Go with her. She can bring Rascal down here and feed him."

Bruce hesitated, prepared to argue his point, but Lillian marched to the door and pushed it open.

"Do you want to wrestle an old lady?" I asked him.

Bruce scowled then got up and followed Lillian out the door.

Paw left his food dish and propped his head on my knee.

"Lillian won the argument." I rubbed his ears.

He closed his eyes and sighed.

A knock on the back door startled me.

"Woof! Woof!" Paw ran to the door.

I pushed him aside with my leg while holding his

collar with one hand and opening the door with my free hand.

Sam Jenkins, one of the town's mail carriers, held out a fistful of mail. "Hey there, Clarissa. Didn't know you were staying here."

"I'm helping the Innsmans for the weekend," I said as he bent forward and scratched Paw's head.

"Hey, big fella." Sam looked up at me. "I heard about that guy dying. Are you investigating?"

"No. Harry is." My detective adventures were well-known, but I didn't want to reveal a current one.

Sam smiled and winked at me. "Got it. Hush. Hush. No problem. I won't say a word."

He handed me the mail. "Give this to Patricia. There's a letter from her sister she'll want to read."

He walked away, whistling in an off-key.

I closed the door. Letter? I snapped my fingers and Paw tilted his head to watch me.

CHAPTER 20

"We need to find Karen," I said to him.

"Why?"

I jumped and turned.

Lillian held Rascal in her arms, staring at me with a curious expression.

"Where's Bruce?"

"Right here," Bruce said as he stepped into the room.

Lillian turned to him. "She says she needs to find Karen, but she hasn't told me why."

"Because Karen had a letter in her coat from Cafferty requesting she meet him here. I want to know why."

"How'd you know she had a letter?"

Bruce answered Lillian. "Because we searched the room before Harry showed up."

Lillian laughed. "Good job." She kissed Rascal. "Okay, boy, let's get you some food before we go find Karen."

Lillian opened a drawer. “Now where is the can opener?”

Behind her back, Bruce waved his arms at me, mouthing, “Keep her here.”

I grimaced. “Lillian...”

“I'm going with you, Bruce Sever.” Lillian scowled at him over her shoulder. “Either you wait for me, or I will follow you.” She grinned toothily at him. “Unless you want to tie me up and lock me in a closet.”

Bruce blanched.

“Lillian,” I began, but she cut me off.

“Same goes for you, Clarissa.”

I sighed. “I was going to tell you that the can opener is on the counter. The electric one. Rascal's food is in the cupboard to your left.”

She hmphed as she opened the cupboard door.

“Mreow.” Rascal rubbed his head against Lillian's chin.

Paw whined.

“You ate your food.” I clipped on his leash. “Let's walk in the garden.”

Lillian cast a suspicious glance my way.

“We won't leave without you. I promise.”

Rascal nudged her chin. “Meow.”

Paw watched the cat but turned and followed me when I tugged on his leash. I grabbed a sweater from the hook by the door. As I turned the knob, Bruce said, “I'll go with you.”

Outside, Bruce took the leash from me as I pulled on my sweater.

Paw sniffed the grass, meandering back and forth. We wandered to a cluster of bushes where Paw watered the ground. He scratched the grass with his back feet, sending clumps of soil and grass at us.

"Paw." I laughed at his antics.

"He's acting like a dog today."

Paw shook himself and leaned against my leg.

"Any idea where to find Karen?" I asked.

"No."

"Maybe we should wait for her to return."

Bruce rubbed the back of his neck. "If she returns."

"You think she won't?"

He shrugged.

"All her stuff is here, including her purse." I frowned. "Is her car in the lot?"

Bruce held up a finger, indicating for me to wait. He jogged around the side of the house.

"Woof!" Paw ran to follow, jerking at the leash.

I held on, barely keeping up. We passed Lillian as she stepped outside.

"Hey!" She said.

I skidded around the corner of the house.

Paw ran between Jac and Shelbee, their arms full of groceries.

I slammed into them.

We tumbled to the grass in a tangle of arms and legs.

I lost my grip on the leash, but Paw turned back to leap into the fray.

We pushed at Paw who pounced on us in play. Food scattered across our legs and rolled across the grass.

"Sit!" Shelbee commanded.

Paw sat.

Lillian picked up his leash and shook her head at us. "You three remind me of the Three Stooges."

Bruce knelt by me. "You okay?"

"I'm fine."

He helped me to my feet.

"We're fine too," Shelbee said as she sat up and surveyed the damage.

Bruce extended a hand, wearing a chagrined expression.

Lillian supported Jac as she stood up.

Canned goods mixed with oranges and apples lay scattered across the grass. At our feet, broken eggs dripped from their carton coating oatmeal spilled from its container.

Paw sniffed at a package of ground beef. "Woof!" He licked and chewed at the wrapper then whined as Lillian and I hauled him away from it.

Shelbee stared at the mess with hands on hips as Jac retrieved the ground beef. "Well...I guess it's back to the grocery store."

She and Jac began cleaning up as I said, "I'll pay for the damaged items."

Jac smiled. "Patricia will appreciate it."

Bruce said, "Her car's in the lot."

"Whose car?" Shelbee asked as she stacked canned goods in a pile.

"Karen's," I said.

"We passed her as we drove home," Jac said. "I'll get a shovel to pick up the oatmeal and eggs."

Shelbee nodded.

"Wait!" I said as Jac was leaving. "Where did you see Karen?"

Shelbee waved Jac on. "She was sitting on a bench outside the coffee shop."

"How long ago was it?" Bruce asked as he reached into his pocket.

"Five maybe ten minutes."

Bruce withdrew his car keys. "Let's go."

I nodded. "Sorry about the mess," I said to her.

Shelbee shrugged. "When Paw's around, mischief happens."

"Woof!"

Bruce had the car running when Paw and I got there. I opened the back door, Paw jumped in, and I followed. Bruce accelerated out of the lot and turned left, speeding down the hill.

He braked when he came upon a slow-moving car. There was no passing on this stretch of the road. Bruce tapped his fingers on the steering wheel as we crawled along.

"We'll find her," I said. "She hasn't any money or identification. She won't get far."

Bruce grunted out a "Maybe."

The driver ahead flicked on their turn signal and turned into the parking lot reserved for the park.

I peered through the windshield as Bruce turned down Curzon then left onto Main. As we passed my house on the left and the pet shop on the right, I watched for Karen. As we neared the coffee shop, I saw her sitting on the bench outside.

"There she is," I said, pointing.

Bruce parked by the curb in front of the hardware store across the street.

I opened my door and Paw jumped out onto the sidewalk. I scurried after him, holding tight to his leash, then slammed the door.

Bruce waited for us in front of the car, took my hand when we joined him, and ushered me across the street.

Karen sat with her head bent, deep in thought. She glanced up with a weary expression when our shadows fell across her.

"What do you want?" she asked.

Tear tracks stained her face. She absently wiped at them with a crumpled tissue.

Paw dropped his head in her lap and gazed at her with big, brown eyes.

She caressed his head with slow strokes. "Why would anyone kill her? She was a kind, good person." Fresh tears trickled down her cheeks.

I sat down beside her while Bruce stuck his hands in his pockets, gazing at the sky.

"I don't know, but we're trying to find out." I pondered how to ask her about the letter we found.

Bruce cleared his throat. "If you want the murderer found, you need to be honest with us."

Karen jerked her chin up and glared at him. "I have been honest."

"Not completely," Bruce said.

I sighed to myself. Bruce pushed too hard.

Karen stiffened beside me and appeared ready to stand up and stalk off, but Paw's head in her lap held her in place. "What are you insinuating?"

Before Bruce could answer, I said, "We found the letter from Cafferty."

She gasped. "You had no right to go through my things."

Bruce crossed his arms. "We had every right. A killer is on the loose."

Karen slumped back against the bench. "I know," she said in a weak voice.

"Did you kill Cafferty?" Bruce asked.

"No."

"But you did come to meet him," I said.

She nodded but didn't say anymore.

"Why? What secret did he threaten to reveal?" I shifted on the bench.

"Our affair. It was years ago. I still don't know how stupid I could have been. I thought I was in love with him. He could be charming when it suited him.

"I waitressed at the coffee shop across from the bank

where Thomas Cafferty worked. I was young and foolishly fell in love with him. Each day he'd eat breakfast and flirt with me, charming me with his wicked grin. I had no idea he was married. Our affair lasted six months; then he tired of me."

She gazed across the street, lost in thought.

A car crossed the center yellow line, angled toward us, and stopped at the curb. Jac sat behind the wheel, and Samuel stuck his head out the back driver-side window which was rolled down. The passenger door opened, and a scowling Lillian got out, slamming the door. She stomped around the car to the sidewalk and waved for Jac to leave.

Jac shrugged, and with a sheepish smile to me, she drove off.

"Yip." Bitsy's head poked above the bottom of the driver's window before Jac drove away.

I held up a hand to stave off Lillian's rant.

Karen shook herself. "I never heard from him again until I received the letter threatening to reveal our affair if I didn't meet him here."

"Why contact you now?" I asked.

"I have a thriving real estate business. My success has landed me lucrative contracts. One of them is for a million-dollar property that Cafferty wanted. He was blackmailing me, threatening to reveal our affair unless I arranged for him to win the bid on the property. A bid that was substantially lower than the property was worth."

"So?" Lillian said. "What's the big deal? An affair isn't a crime. They happen all the time."

Karen frowned. "It may not be a big deal to you but to the people I deal with it is. My reputation is above reproach and it must stay that way. Besides, Cafferty was married to Eleanor Gistal when we had our tryst. The Gistals are wealthy and vindictive. If they found out I was one of Thomas's paramours, they would ruin my career."

"Did you kill him?" Lillian asked.

"No."

"What about Madeline?"

Karen stiffened in offense. "Certainly not. Madeline is —was—my friend. I need to know who killed her as much as you do."

I touched her arm. "Did Madeline know about your affair and the letter?"

"No. I was too embarrassed to tell her." Karen sobbed. "And it's my fault she's dead."

Bruce jerked to attention.

My mouth gaped. "What?"

"Are you confessing to her murder?" Lillian asked.

Karen whipped her head up on a strangled sob. "What? No! I would never harm her." She lowered her head. "Not intentionally."

Her paused stretched long enough for Lillian to say, "Then why is her death your fault?"

"Because I was a coward to face Thomas alone. When I received his letter, I researched Peaceful Dreams and found out they were hosting a murder mystery. Madeline loved mysteries. She'd dragged me to several games in the past. I could never understand her fascination with them. She'd even search for clues as soon as we got to the events."

She stared over at me with red-rimmed eyes. "It was easy for me to convince her to come with me. If I had been braver, I would have met Thomas by myself, and she wouldn't have been here. She wouldn't have been killed."

Karen wept into her tissue.

Lillian shook her head and spoke with a tinge of exasperation in her voice. "Stop blaming yourself. You had no idea a murder would occur."

Karen hiccupped. "I should have voted to end the game instead of supporting Madeline's choice."

Paw whined and raised a paw to Karen's knee.

I loved that my friend showed compassion. "The game may not have anything to do with Cafferty and Madeline's deaths."

"I agree." Bruce studied Karen. "I suggest you go back to the B&B."

"I won't go back to that room."

I placed a hand on her arm. "I'm sure Robert will trade rooms with you. Once Harry releases your old room, my friends will move your belongings to his room."

"What about Madeline's things?"

Bruce rubbed the back of his neck. "Harry should

release anything that he feels isn't connected to her death."

Karen nodded. "I'm tired. I'll sit here for a while then I'll walk back. It's peaceful here."

Bruce jingled his car keys.

I stood up. "We'll go now. If you need someone to talk to, I'd be happy to listen."

Karen squeezed my hand then released it.

"Come on, boy," I said to Paw.

He dropped his paw from her knee, lifted his chin, and stood up. He gazed at Karen a moment then turned and trotted by me as we crossed the street.

Lillian marched by me, grumbling, "This time you aren't leaving me behind."

Bruce opened the front passenger door and bowed to Lillian, who snorted at his actions. While she got in, Paw and I scrambled into the backseat.

Bruce cranked the engine, pulled out into traffic, and drove a block before making a U-turn back toward the B&B.

"Do you believe her?" he asked.

Lillian answered. "Yeah. I do."

"I agree," I said.

"Now what?" Lillian asked.

Bruce tapped his fingers on the steering wheel. He jerked the wheel to the right and parked in a vacant spot along the sidewalk near my house. He stared over his left shoulder, out his window.

I turned, glancing out the rear window, wondering

what he'd seen. On the opposite sidewalk, Donna Dayton strolled with the Innsmans, Henry trotting ahead with his tail in the air.

"Now we talk to Donna," Bruce said. He turned off the car and opened his door while watching her.

Paw jumped across me, eager to get out the back door Bruce held open for me.

By the time I got out, Lillian stood waiting. Bruce took Paw's leash and ruffled his fur. He pointed to Henry. "Look, there's Henry!"

Paw turned his massive head as he followed Bruce's hand. "Woof! Woof!" His joyous bark alerted Henry who strained at his leash. "Woo! Woo!"

Paw ran to the basset, Bruce jogging to keep up.

The Innsmans waved, but Donna ignored us, her arms wrapped around herself.

Paw and Henry met nose to nose and sniffed each other. Their tails wagged at a rapid pace.

From across the street, William chuckled. "I see Henry's made a faithful friend."

Lillian accepted my escort to cross to Bruce.

I smiled at the dogs. "Paw is the friendly sort."

Paw and Henry sniffed an enticing scent and tracked it along the sidewalk.

Patricia hugged Donna with one arm. "We're walking back to make breakfast for Donna."

William glanced at Bruce's car. "Are you going somewhere?"

Bruce thought fast for he said, "We're dropping Lillian

off, but we stopped to pick up cat food." He gestured to the pet shop two doors down.

Patricia raised her eyebrows but didn't contradict Bruce.

Lillian crossed her arms but didn't correct him. Lillian was a well-known frugalist to the locals. No way would she buy high-priced cat food like the pet shop sold. Fortunately, Donna didn't know this fact.

I stepped behind them and moved to Donna's side. "Are you all right?"

Donna lashed out. "Do I look all right?" She sighed. "Sorry. I'm worried about James."

"Uncle has to hold James because he threatened Jessica."

Donna bent her head. "I know," she whispered. "But Jessica provoked him. She's accusing James and me of murder. I know he has a temper, but he wouldn't harm anyone."

Patricia dropped her arm from Donna's shoulder to search her pockets. She withdrew a tissue and blew her nose. "Allergies."

She threw the tissue in one of the trash cans set at intervals along the sidewalk. "Jessica is grieving. Some people lash out when they're hurting."

Donna scowled. "She didn't love him. He was a sugar daddy to her."

"Why would she accuse you and your husband?" Lillian asked.

Donna glared at her. "Because Cafferty poisoned her

mind. He ruined us before and he was determined to do it again."

"How?" I asked.

She blinked at me. "I'm not sure, but after his fight with James, we're certain he planned to discredit us."

Lillian snorted. "Sounds like he was a mean snake."

Donna nodded. "He was."

Patricia adjusted the sleeves of her sweater. "Let's get you some breakfast then you can find a lawyer for James."

Bruce handed Paw's leash to me. "We'll see you back at the B&B."

"See you there," William said as he escorted Patricia and Donna away, Henry lagging.

Paw whined to see his friend leaving.

"Well?" Bruce asked when we were out of hearing range.

"Donna wants Harry to release her husband. She claims James wouldn't hurt anyone and that Cafferty was intent on destroying her and her husband's reputation."

Bruce rubbed his jaw. "Harry won't release James because he threatened Jessica."

"Do you think he hurts Donna?"

"Maybe."

Lillian hmphed. "Do you two brilliant detectives know what you're doing?"

Bruce ignored her sarcasm. "I'm going to the police station."

"I'll come with you."

"Me too," Lillian said.

"Wait," Bruce said. "One of us should return to the B&B."

I crossed my arms and lifted my chin. Paw gazed back and forth between Bruce and me. "And who will that be?"

Lillian laughed. "You, young man, are in trouble. But this time I'll help you." She grasped my arm. "Come on, Clarissa. I'm hungry. We'll go to the B&B." She whispered in my ear. "That's where the murders took place. Better chance to solve them at the scene of the crime."

Paw stood between Bruce and me in a tense stance. I looked down at my dog who picked up on my displeasure with Bruce.

I relaxed my arms. "All right. We'll go to the B&B." I pointed at Bruce. "But you will tell me everything you find out."

Bruce nodded with a slight smirk that I wanted to wipe off his face.

I knew what he was doing. He figured James or Jessica was the murderer and I would be safe at the B&B.

He handed his car keys to me. "I'll see you later." He bent to kiss me, but I turned my cheek.

Whistling to himself, Bruce sauntered down the sidewalk toward the station.

"Come on," Lillian urged me across the street to the car.

"Woof!" Paw ran to the car and hunched down.

"Mreow!"

"Saber?" Lillian crouched to peer under the car.

Paw pushed his head forward. I grabbed his collar

afraid that he would knock Lillian over by accident.

Lillian shoved Paw's shoulder. "Get back you, big galoot! You're scaring my baby."

"Hiss!" Saber assured us that he wasn't scared just displeased.

I opened the front driver side door and threw in a dog treat. Paw regarded it with his head cocked to the side. "Come on, boy. Please get in the car."

He stared at my pleading eyes then rippled his shoulders as if shrugging. With one powerful leap, he jumped onto the front seat and chomped on his treat.

I slammed the door on him.

"Here, Saber. Here, kitty. Come to Momma." Lillian wiggled her fingers at the cat who remained hidden.

"Mreow?"

"Yes. Come here. That old dog is in the car."

Saber slowly poked his head out and gazed from right to left. Once assured it was safe, he strolled to Lillian and rubbed against her knee.

Lillian swooped him up in her arms, kissing the top of his head. "Good boy."

She showered more kisses on the cat who closed his eyes and smiled smugly.

I shook my head at Lillian's behavior. Who knew someone with such a crusty demeanor could be so loving to a cat. I grasped her elbow, assisting her to stand.

Lillian spoke while her nose was buried in Saber's neck fur. "Don't shake your head at me, missy. You're just as bad with Paw."

I smiled. "That's true."

I gazed around the area. Traffic was light this time of day. No cars passed us, which was good because I didn't want Saber to startle and jump from Lillian's arms.

What were we going to do about him? Would Paw ride with Saber in peace?

"I'll walk with Saber." Lillian broke through my thoughts.

"No. It's too far to the B&B or your house."

She harrumphed. "I walked to the B&B from home the other day. I may be older, but I'm active."

I hesitated.

Lillian nudged me with her shoulder. "Go on. We'll meet you there."

I hesitated then shrugged and opened the driver's door, pushing Paw to keep him inside.

"Woof!"

"Hiss!"

I jumped in and slammed my door before cat and dog could interact.

Lillian moved to the sidewalk and walked away. When she was far enough ahead that I felt Saber wouldn't be startled, I cranked the engine.

I drove slowly past her and accelerated up the hill, turning onto Curzon Street, passing Lillian's house. I hoped she would go home, but I doubted it. I turned left on Park Lane and within minutes turned right into the B&B's parking lot and slammed on the brakes.

CHAPTER 21

Mark Carter stood in the middle of the lot staring up at the building.

He jumped out of the path of my car and waved me forward. I pulled up alongside him and rolled down my window.

Mark bent forward and placed his arms on the window frame. "Looks like the police have left. You going to talk to me now?"

Paw pushed his nose through the window from behind my seat. He whined. For some reason, he liked Mark.

I sighed. Mark was persistent which made him a good reporter I suppose. "Yeah. Let me park and we'll talk."

He stood up, and I drove forward and parked in a space at the back of the lot. I unbuckled my belt, got out, and opened Paw's door.

My Saint Bernard jumped down, shook himself with vigor, and woofed at Mark, who ruffled Paw's fur.

"There's my favorite detective dog."

"Woof!" Paw slurped his face.

"Ha! Ha!" Mark wiped the drool from his face with the back of his sleeve. "Sure glad someone appreciates me." He raised an eyebrow at me.

"You," I said, "are as big a ham as he is." I pointed to Paw who waved his tail in a slow happy arc.

"Yes, I am." Mark flipped open his notebook. "And you are as hard to question as your boyfriend."

I held up my hand, palm facing out. "Okay. Ask your questions."

"Aren't you going to invite me inside?" Mark grinned wickedly.

I shook my head. "Fine. We'll go inside."

I turned and strode to the back of the building to the kitchen door. Paw trotted ahead, leading the way.

Mark followed right behind me.

I opened the door and gestured them inside. Paw went first and padded to the dogs' water dish, drinking deeply.

Mark nodded to Paw. "Isn't it against health department rules to have a pet in the kitchen?"

"This is the Innsman's personal kitchen. The commercial kitchen, where they prepare the guests' meals, is across the hall. No pets are allowed in there."

Mark sat at the table in the center of the room. He tapped his notebook on the tabletop.

I sat across from him, and Paw joined me, wetting my pants-leg when he propped his chin on me.

Mark leaned back and crossed his legs out in front of him. "Let's start with who died."

"Don't you already know that?"

He stared at me in silence then said, "I do, but I want to hear your version of events."

I set my hand on Paw's broad head. "Thomas Cafferty was the first person killed. Madeline Wells died last night."

"How?"

"Cafferty fell down the basement stairs."

"Push?"

"Maybe."

Mark looked up from his notebook. "Maybe? I talked to Hal."

I crossed my arms, disturbing Paw who sensed my agitation. "Why ask me if you already know? It's not like you've asked what I saw or did?"

Mark threw down his pen. "Fine. I know Cafferty died from either a blow to the head or a fall down the stairs. Maybe both. What I don't know is why? Or if it is connected to Ms. Wells' death?" He threw his hands up in the air. "I don't even know how she died."

"So?"

"So?" Mark said. "So? How am I to cover crime in this town if no one will talk to me? I've done the background research on the guests. They all had motive, except the Wells woman. Why are they alive and she's not?"

Paw grumbled as I sat up and asked, "Background research? Do you mean what the guests confessed to the other night?"

"No. I did not." A crafty look glinted in his eyes. "I learned quite a bit about your fellow guests. I'll share what I know with you if you answer my questions."

I bit my lip, considering my options.

Bruce and Uncle Harry wouldn't want me to share information with Mark. "What kind of information?"

Mark shook his head. "Uh-uh. I won't share unless you do."

I tapped my fingers on the table as I waited to answer. Perhaps silence would force him to divulge something. We stared at each other, each waiting for the other to break first. Paw sighed and settled against my leg.

Mark threw up his hand in frustration. "All I'll tell you is that there's more to your guests' pasts with Cafferty than they revealed the other night."

I mentally congratulated myself on forcing his hand.

He pointed a finger at me. "Your turn."

"All right. Madeline Wells was smothered to death with a bed pillow."

Mark scribbled in his notebook. "In her bed?"

"Yes."

"Who found her?"

"Karen Taylor. Her roommate."

"What time did it happen?"

I shook my head. "Your turn. What did you learn?"

Mark twirled his pen through his fingers. "Madeline

Wells had no connection to Cafferty, except for knowing Karen Taylor."

"Had she ever met Cafferty before coming to the B&B?"

"Not that I could determine."

I opened my mouth to speak, but Mark held up a hand. "What time did Madeline die?"

"My guess is sometime between midnight and three in the morning."

"Don't you know for certain?"

"No. I do not." I scowled at him. "Ask Hal for his time frame. He's the coroner."

Mark scratched his cheek with his pen. "I figured he'd tell you."

"Well, he didn't. Now, what else did you learn?"

"Karen Taylor had an affair with Cafferty."

I brushed this aside with a wave of my hand. "Already know that."

Mark's eyes widened. "How?"

"She told us."

Mark grunted. "Fine, but did you know that Donna Dayton had an affair with him too?"

My mouth dropped open.

Mark grinned in triumph.

I snapped my mouth shut. "When did they have an affair?"

Paw whined and glanced at the kitchen door. I rubbed his back and he settled down.

"My sources say it was shortly before Cafferty lent

her husband the money for his construction company."

"How long did the affair last?"

"Not long. After James Dayton refused to give Cafferty kickback payments, Donna dropped Cafferty."

"Is that why he set her up to be fired for theft?"

Mark tapped his pen against his notes. "I don't know, but one of my sources claims she wasn't set up."

"Are you saying she embezzled money from the bank?"

"Maybe."

I sat silently for a moment, trying to fit pieces of the puzzle into order.

Mark interrupted my thoughts with a question. "Where was everyone when Madeline was found?"

"I don't know. Patricia and I were in the kitchen when Bruce and Karen came inside."

"Came inside? What time was this?"

"Around three in the morning."

Mark raised an eyebrow. "Why was everybody awake that early in the morning?"

"I don't know why Karen was up. Bruce was patrolling the B&B to protect us from the killer striking again."

Mark grumbled. "Figures."

"What was that?"

Mark waved away my question. "Why were you in the kitchen?"

"I woke up when I heard a sound. I didn't see anyone, but I heard footsteps downstairs, so I went to check it out. I followed the sounds to the kitchen and found Patricia. She said she couldn't sleep and got up to have some tea."

"Where were the others?"

I shook my head. "What else did you learn?"

"Answer my question and I'll answer yours."

I studied him. Mark ignored me, scribbling in his notebook. My best guess was that he only had one more piece of information to tell me. "Shelbee and Jac were sleeping in our room when I left. Patricia told me William was still in their room. I don't know where Donna, James, and Jessica were."

"When did they go to bed?"

I sat back and crossed my arms. Paw grumbled as my movement shifted my thigh under his jaw. "It's your turn."

Mark crossed his arms and stared at me. He waited, hoping I'd start talking, no doubt. I stayed silent.

"Patricia murdered her first husband."

Once again, my mouth dropped open. "What?"

Mark laughed so hard he doubled over. "Got you!"

I closed my mouth and glared at him. "That's not funny!"

Mark drew in a deep breath. "You should have seen your face." He coughed. "Seriously, I know nothing about Patricia's first marriage. As far as I can tell she had a happy one, unlike me."

"You were married?"

Mark sat up. "That's none of your business."

I nodded. "Okay. Did you learn anything else about the guests?"

"One thing. Cafferty was going to propose to Jessica according to my sources. This would be her third marriage. Both of her previous husbands died suddenly."

"Are you serious?"

"Yes. Her first husband died in his sleep. He was a young man. The autopsy ruled his death a heart attack."

"Could Jessica have poisoned him?"

"If she did, it didn't show in the autopsy."

"How long were they married?"

"A year."

I shivered. "A short marriage."

Mark nodded. "So was the second one. Her second husband died in a car accident a year and a half into the marriage. His brakes failed."

Ring!

I jerked at the sound of the phone on the kitchen wall.

"Woof!" Paw trotted over and sat staring up at the phone, head tilted to the side.

Ring! Ring!

I hurried over to the phone and lifted the receiver. "Hello?"

Bruce's voice sounded relieved. "Glad it's you. Harry arrested Jessica."

"Why?"

Mark joined me to eavesdrop on the conversation. "What did he say?"

"Who's that?" Bruce asked with a hint of suspicion.

"Mark Carter."

Bruce grunted.

Mark nudged me. "What did he tell you?"

Bruce heard Mark's question. "The Chief arrested Jessica. She confessed to planting that pen in Donna's purse to throw suspicion on the Daytons."

"What pen," Mark asked as I said, "Why arrest her?"

Bruce ignored Mark's question. "James Dayton wanted to press charges against Jessica. She, in turn, is refusing to drop charges against him."

Mark waved his hands in the air, trying to get my attention.

Paw stared at Mark with a curious expression.

"Hold on a minute," I told Bruce. I turned to Mark. "Paw found a pen in Donna Dayton's purse that was engraved with Cafferty's name. Jessica swears its Cafferty's and that he lost it. And James threatened Jessica with a chair leg. That was before the pen incident."

Mark gaped at me. "And you didn't mention this to me?"

"You didn't tell me everything," I said.

Bruce cleared his throat. "Harry's holding them both. He's waiting to find evidence to arrest Jessica for Cafferty's murder."

I glanced at Mark. "Harry needs to talk with Mark. He discovered that Jessica'd been married twice. Both men died suddenly."

Bruce whistled. "Send him down to the station."

I raised a brow at Mark who was eavesdropping on the call.

"Tell your boyfriend that I'm heading there now." He strode across the kitchen and opened the door.

"Mark's leaving. He'll be there shortly."

"Good. Could you find Donna and ask her to come to the station too? Harry wants to ask her some questions about Jessica."

"I'll find her."

Bruce murmured endearments and hung up.

The outside door rattled, and Lillian entered with Saber in her arms.

Paw ran over to them, tail wagging. "Woof! Woof!"

"Mrrow! Hiss!"

"Get away, you, galoot!"

I rushed over, grabbed Paw's collar, and tugged him back. He resisted, eager to sniff Saber.

I tightened my grip on Paw's leash. "Let him alone, Paw."

Paw whined and jerked, attempting to free himself.

"Meow!"

Lillian, Saber, Paw, and I turned at the sound. Rascal stood in the kitchen doorway, regarding us with a quizzical expression.

Saber and Paw stopped fussing and stared in silence at the new arrival.

"Where did he come from?" Lillian wondered.

"Didn't you leave him in the kitchen when you left?"

"Sure, but Shelbee said she'd take him up to Patricia's apartment."

"Maybe she forgot. But, where is she?"

Lillian shrugged. "Don't know. Jac was going to the store to replenish the supplies Paw ruined after she dropped me off with you."

"Hmm. Well, I'll check on her after I talk with Donna. Although come to think of it, I haven't seen her or the Innsmans. They should have been back by now."

Lillian shrugged. "Go look for them and take the big galoot with you."

"What are you going to do?" I asked.

"Feed Saber."

"Mreow." Saber licked his nose with his pink tongue.

"Meow?" Rascal strolled over, tail held high, and rubbed against Lillian's leg.

Paw whined and gazed up at me, asking permission to join the cats.

"Come on, boy. Let's find Donna and the others."

With a gentle tug, I coaxed Paw from the kitchen, closing the door behind me. I stepped across the hall, pushed open the commercial kitchen's door, and peeked inside. No one was in sight, and no food smells wafted in the air.

"Where are Donna and Patricia?" I spoke to Paw. "They should be back by now."

Paw whined and shifted restlessly on his feet.

"Let's check in front." I led him into the foyer and crossed to the living room. Again, no one was in sight.

Paw turned and tugged me toward the stairs. I followed as he led the way up and stopped on the first landing. He stood with head cocked on the side, listening. He swung his head to the left and softly woofed, then took a few steps forward and glanced at me over his shoulder.

"Lead the way, boy."

He led me to Donna's room and scratched at the door.

"Stop that," I scolded him. "You'll ruin the Innsman's wood finish."

He stopped and looked up with a wounded expression.

Ignoring his sad eyes, I knocked on the door.

Rustling sounded along with footsteps as someone approached, then the door was inched open. Donna peered around the door. "Yes?"

"Sorry to bother you, but Bruce called me. He asked me to tell you that they want you to go to the police station."

Donna sucked in a breath, her eyes widening. "Why? Are they releasing James?"

"No. Could I come in a minute to explain?"

She paused then opened the door wider and stood back.

I stepped in, Paw behind me.

Donna turned her back and walked to the bed where a suitcase sat open, half-filled with rumpled clothes. "Why do they want me at the station?" Donna asked over her shoulder as she rummaged in the suitcase.

"The police have arrested Jessica for planting his pen in your purse. They want to ask you some questions about her."

Donna's shoulders relaxed and she half-turned toward me. "I knew she was trying to pin Cafferty's murder on us. Did she murder him?"

"I don't know." From the corner of my eyes, I saw Paw's body tense. *What had upset him?* His nose lifted, scenting the air.

"I bet she did." Donna sat on the edge of the bed. "Maybe they'll release James now."

"Maybe."

Donna scrutinized me. "You don't believe they will."

"No. James threatened Jessica with that chair leg. We all witnessed it. Even if she did murder Mr. Cafferty, James will be tried for his actions."

Donna's face hardened. "He's a fool sometimes." She stood up and turned back to her packing.

Paw moved to stand in front of me. Something was wrong. He growled low in his throat.

Donna tensed at the sound and glanced at me over her shoulder. "Call your dog off."

I studied her hard expression. "Paw is a good judge of character."

She snorted and turned.

Pointing a pistol at my heart. "He's a pain in my butt."

CHAPTER 22

I took a deep breath.

"Call him off, or I'll put a bullet in him." She lowered the pistol to point at Paw.

I tugged very gently on his leash. "Paw."

His gaze never left Donna's face.

I tugged harder. "It's okay, boy. Back off."

Continuing to stare at Donna, he eased back to my side.

"You killed Cafferty."

She smirked. "He fell down the stairs."

"But with help."

She shrugged. "Thomas was a fool. Greedy too. He found James in the basement, retrieving the wine bottle for me."

I frowned. "Why did you want it?"

"The Chateau Haut Brion is remarkable. I've tasted it once before. Why should Innsman or Thomas have it?"

Paw shifted.

Donna tensed.

I stroked Paw's side to soothe him, afraid Donna would shoot him.

"What happened when Cafferty found James?"

Her gazed shifted back to me. "They argued. I was waiting in the dining room as a lookout. I saw Thomas go past me. He met James on the stairs as James was at the bottom of the steps, first foot on the step with the bottle in hand.

"Thomas stopped at the top and threatened to inform the Innsmans unless James handed over the bottle. He never heard me move up behind him. I hit him over the head with my pistol. He fell, and James jumped back."

"He was dead."

"Yes," she said, no feeling to her voice. "Broke his neck."

"How did the wine bottle end up in the mulch?"

Donna sighed. "We heard footsteps coming down the main stairs. James panicked. He wanted to leave the bottle, but I refused, so he rushed us up the stairs and out the back door. I hid the gun in a hidden compartment in our car while he hid the wine. Idiot. Who hides fine wine in a mulch pile?"

Her cold gaze bored into me. "Time to go."

She motioned with the pistol. "Lock him in the closet."

The door to her bedroom closet stood partially open. Items of clothing hung amongst the empty hangers.

I glanced around the room, desperate to find something with which to hit her. I dared not scream for fear Lillian would come upstairs to help me. Donna would shoot her.

"Stop dawdling!" Donna trained her gun on Paw. "Or I'll shoot him here."

Resigned, I tugged on Paw's leash. "Come on boy."

Paw refused to move as his gaze remained locked on the gun.

"Move, mutt, or I'll put a bullet in your mistress."

Paw growled low in his throat, so I crouched next to him to calm him, fearing Donna would pull the trigger.

I whispered to him. "Go in the closet. Escape as soon as you can."

He turned his head so that one eye watched me while the other tracked Donna's movements.

He whined softly.

"Stop talking and get him moving." Donna's voice held a note of desperation.

I stood up and tugged the leash.

Paw followed me to the closet and waited as I pushed the door wider. He balked at going inside, but I shoved his butt to get him moving.

When he was inside, I pushed the door shut with an audible click. The closet door didn't have a lock, but my heart sank when I saw the round doorknob. Paw could open a lever-style handle but not a knob.

I turned around to face Donna. She motioned with the gun to her suitcase. "Close it and pick it up. You're going with me."

I went to the bed and folded the suitcase closed, latching it.

Paw scratched furiously at the closet door.

Donna moved over to it, and keeping the gun trained on me, banged on the door. "Stop that!"

Paw ceased.

Donna picked up her purse from the top of the dresser and motioned to the door with the gun. "Let's go."

I lifted the suitcase and walked out of the room with Donna right behind me. She closed the door to the room but didn't lock it. It, too, had a knob lock.

I breathed deeply to quell my rising panic. I was on my own because Paw couldn't get out, but at least he was safe. The suitcase was too heavy for me to swing it around and hit her.

"Clarissa? Where are you?"

Oh no! Lillian.

Donna growled, "Tell her to go away."

How was I to get rid of Lillian? I knew if I told her to go she'd refuse.

"I'm up here, Lillian. I'm helping Donna, but I'll be down in a minute."

Donna urged me to continue walking, and we advanced to the head of the stairs.

At the bottom, Lillian stood with arms crossed and demanded, "Have you seen Rascal?"

Rascal? Oh, the cat.

Donna shoved the gun into my back. She whispered, "Get rid of her."

I looked down at Lillian. "No, but I'll look for him as soon as I'm done helping Donna."

Lillian hmphed and climbed up the stairs.

I panicked. "Lillian, I'll do it. Why don't you see if Jac is back?"

Lillian continued to climb, saying, "Jac's not back and I'll check for Rascal. He was here a moment ago."

She stopped halfway up and turned as the front door opened and Bruce rushed inside.

He saw Lillian and gazed past her to me. "Clarissa, sweetheart, can you come here and help me? You too, Lillian."

Donna moved the gun to my neck. "Stay where you are."

Lillian scowled. "Let her go."

"Shut up, old woman."

Lillian drew herself up to her full height. "Old woman?"

Bruce said, "Let her go, Mrs. Dayton."

Donna laughed. "Now why would I do that? She's my ticket out of here."

Bruce moved forward, and Donna pointed the gun at him while grasping my arm to hold me in place. "One more move and I'll shove her down the stairs. My guess is she'll take the old woman down with her."

"Grr."

Donna jerked at the sound of Paw's growl behind her and half turned, swinging the gun in his direction. "How—"

Everything happened in a blur.

Paw launched himself up and clamped his jaws around Donna's gun wrist.

She screamed, dropping the gun, and shoved me, the suitcase swinging forward, pulling me down the stairs. As I fell, a black blur whizzed past my head.

Donna's screams intensified.

A heavy weight slammed into my chest pushing me backwards, where I landed in a heap on the landing behind me. Dazedly, I looked up into Samuel's face. He turned toward Paw who continued his hold on Donna's wrist.

Donna raised her free hand to hit Saber who was attacking her head.

Samuel clamped onto that hand.

Bruce ran to me, yelling, "Lillian, calm Saber."

I heard Lillian say, "Get her, Saber."

Bruce groaned, knelt next to me. "Sweetheart?"

"I'm okay. Get Donna."

I lay on the floor watching the action. Lillian called Saber who jumped off Donna's head and hissed, prepared to attack again.

Samuel allowed Bruce to push him back so that Bruce could grab Donna's arm.

Paw held onto Donna's wrist, the gun lying a few feet

away. He released his hold when Bruce praised him and urged him away.

Bruce grabbed Donna's wrist. Bruce flipped Donna over, pinning her arms behind her.

Harry, who I hadn't seen come in, trudged up the stairs and handcuffed Donna.

He lifted Donna to her feet as she resisted him, struggling, kicking, and cursing.

Officer Heldman ran up the stairs and assisted Harry in restraining Donna as Harry read her rights.

Lillian scooped up Saber who washed his paws with swipes from his tongue. He nestled in her arms and purred in contentment.

Donna cursed the cat. "That thing attacked me. Get me a doctor. I'll have that animal and those dogs put down."

Lillian bristled. "You'll do no such thing. You're a spiteful woman." She cuddled Saber close to her chest and glared at Donna.

Paw ignored Donna and brushed past everyone to come to my side, slurping my face.

I hugged him tightly. "I'm okay, boy. Thanks to you."

He nudged me with his head and panted happily, as I scratched his ears.

Bruce bagged the gun and handed it to Harry.

Jac rushed up the stairs with Bitsy racing ahead. The little dog ran up to Donna and peed on her leg.

"Argh! Get me away from these mutts!"

Harry laughed. "You deserve far worse. Come on. We're going to the station."

Heldman led Donna down the stairs and out the door to his patrol car.

Harry looked down at me. "You all right?"

I nodded.

"Good. I need your statement."

William skidded through the front door, slamming it behind him. "What happened?"

"Woo! Woo!" Henry dropped his nose to the foyer floor and trailed a scent.

William studied us. "Where's Patty?"

Bruce frowned. "What do you mean? I thought she was with you and Donna."

Jac asked, "Where's Shelbee?"

"And Rascal," Lillian added.

"Who's Rascal?" Harry asked.

"Our cat," William said as he strode toward the kitchens. "Patty has to be here. I left her with Donna when I took Henry with me to make an appointment for Donna with a lawyer."

"Wait!" Jac called to William. "Henry smells something."

The basset, ears dragging the floor, bayed softly as he tracked a scent across the foyer, heading to the front door.

Bruce extended a hand to me and levered me to my feet. Leaving Donna's suitcase on the landing, the group of us descended the stairs. Paw, Samuel, and Bitsy added their noses to the hunt, but it was clear by Henry's determined focus that he was the better tracker.

Saber remained in Lillian's arms, regarding the dogs with feline disdain.

Henry led us to the front door. "Woo! Woo!"

"Woof! Woof!"

"Yip! Yip!"

"Woof!" Paw glanced back at me then pushed next to Henry and clamped his mouth over the doorknob.

"I'll open it," Bruce said, but I raised my hand in a staying motion.

Slowly, Paw turned the knob and the door clicked open. Henry shoved his muzzle in the gap and pushed through, nose to the ground.

Bruce glanced at me with wide eyes. "Since when can he open a round knob?"

I smiled, proud of my pooch. "Since he needed to save me."

"Huh," Bruce said.

Lillian poked him in the side. "Get going. I wanna see where that dog is leading us."

Bruce wrapped an arm around my shoulders and bowed Lillian through the door.

She sniffed audibly as she passed him.

"Woo! Woo!" Henry increased his pace, tail wagging like a metronome.

Paw and Samuel eased their longer strides to match the basset's shorter ones.

Paw gazed back at me. "Woof!"

Bitsy stood up against Jac's leg who picked her up carrying her with us.

Our group trooped around the house to the back and across the lawn in the dogs' wake, heading toward a garden shed in the back corner of the garden.

Henry trailed the scent to the doors of the shed, stood up on hind legs, and pushed at the doors. He bayed as he scratched at the door panels.

"Oh no! He's found something." William reached toward the door's padlock, but Harry grabbed his arm.

"Wait!" He pulled gloves from his belt pouch and stripped them on then grasped the lock with care. "You have the key for this."

"Yeah, but it's usually left unlocked."

"It's locked now."

William blanched, turned, and pounded on the doors. "Patty! Are you in there? Answer me?"

Muffled thumping sounded from within.

"I'll get the key!" Jac set Bitsy on the ground and tore across the lawn. Bitsy yipped and followed her, thinking it was a game.

Paw and Samuel, noses to the grass, sniffed around the shed as William placed his ear to the door and Henry scratched at the bottom of the door.

Bruce and Harry shared an uneasy glance which caused my stomach to drop.

Would we find one of our friends dead inside?

CHAPTER 23

The scrabbling sounds indicated someone was alive though.

Jac raced up and handed the key to Harry who inserted it, popping the padlock open. He removed the lock but was shoved aside as William flipped the latch and jerked the door open.

"Patty!" William rushed inside and knelt by a prone figure.

Patricia lay on her side, hands and feet bound, duct tape over her mouth.

To her left, Shelbee lay still, bound and gagged as well.

"No!" Jac and I cried and hurried to her side. Samuel and Bitsy pushed in between us, nuzzling her.

Rip!

Patricia cried out in pain, exclaiming, "That hurts" when her duct tape was removed.

Jac felt for a pulse at Shelbee's neck and blew out a sigh. "She's alive."

I blinked back tears. "Can you see an injury?"

From behind me, Patricia spoke in a muffled voice. "Donna---back---"

I glanced over to see her embraced in William's arms, Henry burrowing between them.

William eased his hold enough for her to raise her head from his chest.

"Donna hit Shelbee on the back of the head with her pistol." She sobbed and nestled back into William's embrace.

I felt through Shelbee's hair searching for her injury as Harry stepped outside and radioed for emergency assistance.

I brushed against a sizable lump causing Shelbee to groan.

Jac tore the duct tape from her mouth bringing Shelbee fully awake with a curse. She attempted to sit up but slumped back down. "Dizzy," she mumbled.

"Lie still," I said, working to release her wrist bindings.

Samuel chewed at her foot bindings while Bitsy licked her face.

"Hey, sweetheart," Shelbee mumbled to her. "What happened?"

Patricia sat up with her back to the wall. "Donna hit you over the head."

"Why?" Shelbee gusted out on a pained breath.

"That I don't know."

Bruce brushed Samuel aside to assist with Shelbee's bindings.

Samuel whined, refusing to abandon Shelbee. He stepped on my legs and pushed to get closer.

Harry stepped back into the shed. "Tell me what happened."

"Donna and I met Shelbee on the front steps when we returned to the B&B. She was going out here to get a flower pot for me." Patricia sniffled. "It's my fault she was hurt."

Shelbee raised her head an inch and said, "No, it's not. It's Donna's fault."

"She's right," William said as Jac nodded in agreement.

"Go on," Harry said to Patricia. "Why the flower pot?"

"It's for one of the shut-ins the church visits. The lady's birthday is next week, and I bought a flower for her, but I'm repotting it first. I mentioned it to Shelbee, and she offered to find a pot in the shed."

Shelbee mumbled. "Forgot with all the events going on. Just thought of it today."

"Why were you going out the front door?" I asked.

"Because I heard you and Mark coming in the kitchen. I didn't want to interrupt."

Bruce said, "You mean you didn't want to talk to Mark again."

I shot Bruce a scowl, but Shelbee smirked, "That too."

"All right," Harry said, "let's get back to what happened." He nodded for Patricia to explain.

Sirens wailed in the distance.

Patricia rubbed her wrists. "I told Donna to go inside, and I'd fix her breakfast after I helped Shelbee choose a flowerpot. Shelbee and I were in the shed when Donna joined us. Our backs were to her, and as she stepped in, we turned toward her. She raised a gun and slammed it down on Shelbee's head."

Sirens wailed loudly as they drew closer and I heard tires screech as they entered the parking lot. Doors slammed amid raised voices.

Patricia drew a ragged breath. "Shelbee collapsed, and Donna pointed the gun at me, ordering me to tie up Shelbee. She threw a roll of duct tape at me. If I didn't comply, she threatened to kill Shelbee, so I tied her up then wrapped tape around my ankles. Donna taped my wrists, checked that the tape I wrapped was tight, and gagged both of us. She taped my wrists to my ankles, did the same to Shelbee, then closed the door and locked it."

William cursed.

The EMTs pushed into the shed, one going to Shelbee as the other knelt by Patricia.

Harry motioned everyone out, but William refused to leave.

"Clarissa," William asked, "take Henry, will you?"

I nodded and picked up his leash, giving it a gentle tug. "Come on, Henry."

He refused to move.

"Paw," I said to my Saint who waited by the door, "help me with Henry."

"Woof."

Henry, a mulish expression in his sad eyes, stood up and slowly stepped forward.

"Let's go, Paw," I said, giving him a gentle nudge.

Jac picked up Bitsy as Bruce tugged Samuel away from Shelbee. Both dogs whined and struggled to get back to Shelbee's side.

Paw trotted out without complaint and Henry plodded behind. They sat beside Lillian who had remained outside with Saber in her arms.

Harry drew me aside. "Give me a quick rundown of what happened with Donna."

I recounted my confrontation with her.

"She never mentioned Ms. Wells?"

"No," I said, "but I'm sure she and James are responsible."

Harry's police radio squawked. "Chief?"

Harry keyed it on. "Yeah?"

"You better get back here. The Daytons are screaming at each other." In the background, I could hear a woman's raised voice.

"I'm on my way." Harry strode away toward the parking lot.

I rejoined Shelbee who was strapped to a gurney, protesting, "I'm fine."

Jac crossed her arms. "You're going to the hospital and be checked out."

Lillian asked, "Where's Rascal?"

Jac's mouth dropped open. "Is that all you can think

about?"

Shelbee waved a hand at Lillian. "He's fine. I took him up to the apartment before going to the shed."

"Hmph." Lillian turned and marched to the house, Saber in her arms.

William hugged Patricia as he escorted her outside. "You should go too."

Patricia shook her head. "I'm stiff from being tied up, but I wasn't hurt."

Henry trotted over and leaned against her side.

As the EMTs loaded Shelbee onto the ambulance, Samuel jumped in.

"Hey, he can't be in here," Rob said. The EMT pointed to the mastiff. "Someone remove him."

Bruce jumped in and tugged at Samuel's collar, but the dog refused to move.

Shelbee spoke to Samuel. "It's okay, sweetheart. I'll be fine. Stay with Clarissa."

"But I'm going with you," I said.

"No. Keep Samuel and Bitsy with Paw. Jac can pick me up at the hospital."

Seeing my frown, Shelbee smiled. "You handle Mark better than we do."

I growled, causing Paw to tilt his head, curious as to why I sounded like him. "Coward," I teased her.

She smirked then winced and rubbed her temple.

Paw gazed between us and woofed to Samuel, who jumped out of the ambulance.

"Let's go," Rob said.

Bruce stepped out of the vehicle and held onto the mastiff.

Jac strode to her car in the parking lot. I picked up Bitsy before she could follow as the ambulance drove away.

Bruce, Patricia, William, and I stood in silence with the dogs at our feet.

"She's going to be all right," I said out loud to convince myself.

Bruce released Samuel and hugged me. "She will."

"Shelbee's tough." Patricia stretched her shoulders. "That's why Donna hit her. She struck before Shelbee saw her, otherwise, Shelbee could have knocked the gun from her hand."

"I wonder..." Bruce stared off into the distance.

I nudged his side. "What?"

He looked down at me. "Did she kill Madeline?"

"I don't know, but perhaps Uncle Harry will find out."

CHAPTER 24

Shelbee spent several hours at the hospital and returned to the B&B shortly after dinner. I hadn't seen or heard from my uncle since he returned to the station. Patricia insisted Shelbee stay at the B&B where she could be properly cared for until she fully recovered. Jac, who had gone home from the hospital to check on her dad, returned to spend the night as well. Bruce suggested he and I stay too.

I raised an eyebrow. "Do you think a killer is still on the loose?"

He scratched the stubble on his chin. "No, but I feel responsible for Shelbee's wellbeing."

"Neither of us suspected Donna," I said. "Don't hold onto guilt."

Stubbornly, he said, "I'm staying at the inn tonight."

I didn't protest because I had already sworn to stay by

Shelbee's side until she recovered. Bruce wasn't the only one feeling guilty.

Karen returned to the inn and moved to Shelbee and Jac's room on the third floor. Robert returned home so Jac and Shelbee could have his room. Fewer stairs for Shelbee to climb.

No one wanted to sleep in the room where Madeline had been murdered.

Bruce and I slept in the living room along with Paw. Bruce spent the night patrolling but in the early hours collapsed on the sofa across from me. He and Paw serenaded me with their snoring.

I gave up trying to sleep around seven in the morning when Jac tiptoed down the stairs. I met her in the foyer.

"Let's walk the dogs," she whispered to me. "Shelbee's sleeping."

I nodded agreement, and with Paw, Samuel, and Bitsy frisking ahead, walked to the front door.

The phone rang one ring.

Jac grabbed my arm. "William will get it."

I snapped on Paw's leash while Jac did the same for Samuel and Bitsy. We then stepped outside and walked around back to the garden.

Neither of us spoke as the dogs hurried to do their business. We hustled in the back door to the smell of fresh coffee.

"Good morning," Patricia said from across the room. She filled cups for Jac and I. "Clarissa, Harry called. He wants to meet with everyone in an hour. Can you two help me prepare breakfast?"

"Of course." Jac gulped coffee.

"Karen is joining us so use the commercial kitchen to cook." Patricia gestured to Jac. "I'll join you as soon as I fix Henry's breakfast.

Jac left, and I asked, "Where is he?"

"Henry?"

I nodded.

"William is walking him down to the bakery to get some pastries."

"I'll feed Paw, Samuel, and Bitsy."

Patricia waved me away. "Go help Jac. I'll feed them." She opened a cupboard, bent down, pulled out three cans of dog food, and stood up. All three dogs rushed to sit in front of her. Paw ignored me in favor of food, and I slipped out and crossed to the other kitchen.

Uncle Harry arrived an hour later with Lillian. "Found her walking up the hill."

Lillian rolled her eyes.

I placed the last fork on the table. "Where's Saber?"

"At home. He's sitting in the window watching the birds at my new bird feeder."

The dining room table was set with plates, glasses, and utensils. Jac and Patricia carried the last dishes of food into the room.

Shelbee sat at the table with a grumpy frown, irritated that we wouldn't let her help. Dark shadows smudged under her eyes and she moved her head cautiously.

Karen sat to Shelbee's left, a crumpled tissue in her hand and a haggard expression on her face.

William motioned everyone to a seat while he sat at the head of the table. Patricia sat to his left and Harry to his right. Bruce and I sat across from each other with Jac to my right.

"You look tired, Uncle."

He smiled weakly and patted my shoulder. "It's been a long night."

"Then dig in and eat," Patricia said as she passed him a platter of pancakes.

We passed pancakes, scrambled eggs, sausage, bacon, and toast around the table. Bruce poured orange juice into Shelbee's glass.

Murmurs of approval and compliments to Jac and Patricia on their cooking mingled with stretches of silence as we ate.

Harry devoured his pancakes then wiped his mouth with his napkin and sat back, cradling his cup of coffee. "If no one minds, I'll explain what happened after I left yesterday while you eat." He covered a deep yawn with his hand.

Several of us nodded our consent.

"When I got back to the station, the Daytons were engaged in a shouting match. Between their mutual threats, arguments, and confessions, I concluded that they were the killers of both Cafferty and Ms. Wells."

Karen stifled a sob with her tissue.

"They confessed?" Bruce finished a forkful of eggs.

"Yes." Harry gulped coffee. "James accused Donna of masterminding the murders. That betrayal, as she called it, caused her to confess to her husband's part in the murders."

Harry popped a grape into his mouth and chewed.

I shifted in my chair. "So what she told me was true? She hit Cafferty over the head when he confronted James on the basement stairs?"

"Yeah. She did. I talked with Mark Carter. The information he dug up helped to get her confession. Apparently, she did embezzle money from the bank she worked at because her husband's construction business was ruined, thanks to Cafferty. That's when Cafferty blackmailed her.

"If she agreed to be his mistress, he wouldn't press charges. She refused, and he had her fired. She's held a grudge ever since. They were planning on killing Cafferty but not that night.

"James tried to steal the wine bottle, so they could sell it. When Cafferty interrupted, Donna saw her chance to end him. She showed no remorse, except that Paw found the wine bottle in the mulch, ruining her chances of stealing it."

Harry shook his head at their callous nature.

William smirked. "They would have been fooled if they had gotten the wine. That bottle was a fake."

Patricia lay her hand on the back of William's hand. "What about Madeline?" She asked Harry.

"They killed her, too." Harry paused as Karen sobbed harder.

"Why?" Jac asked.

Harry turned to me. "Why do you think?"

I opened my mouth but paused before speaking. Why did they murder Madeline? Shelbee lay down her knife across her plate sparking an idea. "The clues. Madeline was searching for them at night. They must have thought she saw them."

"Clues?" Lillian asked.

"Yes," Karen said, wiping her eyes. "Madeline loved to beat out the competition at mystery games. She'd get up in the middle of the night and search for clues. I told her not to do it. That it was cheating, but she'd laugh and say all was fair in a game." Fresh tears tracked down her cheeks.

Harry nodded. "Donna confessed that Madeline was sneaking around the B&B the night they killed Cafferty." He held up his hands at Karen's protest. "Her words, not mine."

Harry cleared his throat. "Donna ripped that wooden wine bottle out of Madeline's hands and scared her up to bed with threats of informing the Innsmans, who would kick her out of the game. Donna dropped the wooden bottle in the confrontation with Cafferty. They panicked when they thought someone was coming."

Bruce sat back and crossed his arms. "Did Madeline confront Donna after Cafferty's death?"

"Yes. According to James, Madeline spoke with Donna

and told her she would tell the police about the wooden bottle that Donna took from her if Donna didn't. James claims Donna wanted to tie up loose ends and forced him to hold Madeline while she smothered her. Donna says that James did it."

Karen jumped up and rushed from the room.

Patricia started to follow, but Harry waved her back to her seat. "Let her go for now."

Bruce pointed to Harry. "Who do you think smothered Madeline?"

"Both of them. My guess is James held her down while Donna smothered her."

Shelbee hugged herself. "Why didn't she kill Patricia and me?"

Harry gazed at her sympathetically. "Probably because a gunshot would have drawn attention. Appears as though she was leaving town without James. That's one of the reasons James talked. He was furious when he realized she was skipping out on him."

I tapped the table with my fingertips. "The fake weapon we found in Madeline's room. She must have found it in her nighttime search."

Bruce nodded. "Probably."

William refilled his coffee cup, asking, "What about Jessica?"

Harry grunted. "She refused to answer any further questions until she speaks with her lawyer, however, she admitted planting the pen. Oddly, she was correct in her suspicions of James and Donna killing Cafferty."

Shelbee sipped her juice then asked, "Why didn't the Daytons target Jessica? I mean she was the one who kept accusing them of murder."

Harry set down his coffee. "Maybe they did but didn't have a chance to attack her. Jessica told me she wedged a chair under her doorknob. She was paranoid that the Daytons would sneak into her room and kill her."

William scratched his jaw. "How did they get in Madeline's room?"

"Donna picked the lock. We found a lock picking kit in her suitcase."

"Woof! Woof!"

"Woo! Woo!"

I jumped up. "Sounds like the dogs want to join us."

"Not before we clear the table," Patricia said. "Is everyone finished?"

Everyone was so Patricia and Jac stacked dishes and platters.

Shelbee stood up to help, but Jac pushed her to sit back down. "You rest."

Lillian patted Shelbee's hand. "Don't worry. I'll keep you company."

Shelbee smiled weakly.

Harry swigged the last of his coffee. "Time for me to leave." He turned to me. "Walk me out."

I nodded, but instead of heading for the front door, Harry strode to the kitchen where the dogs were. He entered to a chorus of barks and yips.

The dogs milled around us. Harry scratched Paw

between the ears. "I'm proud of you, boy. Once again you saved our Clarissa."

"Woof!" Paw gazed at Harry with his tongue lolling out.

"Come on." Harry led me outside but closed the door on the dogs who tried to follow.

He settled a heavy hand on my shoulder. "You know I love you, right?"

I nodded.

"Then please try to stay out of trouble, okay? I don't want to lose my favorite niece."

I stood on tiptoe and kissed his cheek. "I'll try, Uncle. I'll try."

He nodded and strolled away.

Turning to the door, I spied Bruce standing there with arms crossed, Paw sitting at his feet.

He enveloped me in a huge bear hug. "My heart stopped when I saw Donna pointing that gun at your head."

"I wasn't happy about it either," I quipped.

He drew back enough to look down into my eyes. "Please be more careful."

I opened my mouth to protest that I was careful, but he hushed me with a finger to my lips. "I love you."

I smiled and kissed his finger. "I love you too."

Paw wedged his head between us. "Woof!"

We laughed, and I said, "I love you too, Paw!"

REVIEW REQUEST

THANK you for reading. I truly appreciate your taking time from your busy day to read my novel. I know your time is limited, but could you do me a favor? Could you leave a review of this story? Reviews are an important part of a writer's marketing success.

Please see the *About the Author* page to contact Ms. Baublitz, and don't forget to sign up for the newsletter on her site to be the first to get updates on upcoming publications!

ABOUT THE AUTHOR

SANDRA Baublitz is a lover of all animals. She has always loved dogs and cats. A Dog Detective series originally began as a contest entry. Paw's creation was influenced by the Beethoven movies and the author's desire to own a Saint Bernard. The author never got the opportunity to own a St. Bernard and her current cats will not allow a new edition. Ms. Baublitz expresses her love of the breed by continuing to write about Clarissa and Paw and their mystery adventures. She hopes her readers enjoy reading them as much as she enjoys writing them.

Please don't forget to sign up for the newsletter on her site to be the first to get updates on upcoming publications!

sandrabaublitz.com

OTHER BOOKS BY SANDRA BAUBLITZ

SHORT STORIES:

The Mystery of the Blue Dolphins

The Mystery of Aunt Carol's Disappearance

The Mystery of the Body in the Shed

The Mystery of the Missing Bear

The Mystery of the Missing Actor

SHORT STORY COLLECTION:

A Dog Detective Short Story Collection (Books 1-5)

NOVELS:

Mastiffs, Mystery, and Murder

Printed in Dunstable, United Kingdom

72653800R00180